THE · ANYWHERE · RING

CASTLE IN TIME

Louise Ladd

D0067509

BERKLEY BOOKS, NEW YORK

CASTLE IN TIME

A Berkley Book / published by arrangement with
the author

PRINTING HISTORY
Berkley edition / November 1995

ISBN: 0-425-15048-8

BERKLEY®
Berkley Books are published by The Berkley Publishing Group,
200 Madison Avenue, New York, New York 10016.
BERKLEY and the "B" design
are trademarks belonging to Berkley Publishing Corporation.

PRINTED IN THE UNITED STATES OF AMERICA

10 9 8 7 6 5 4 3 2 1

"Stephen, where are you?"

My voice seemed to dissolve into the thick dark mist. I took a few steps uphill, moving only as far as the flashlight beam lit the way, stopping, then taking a few more steps. BOOM! A huge rolling blast of thunder shook me. A few moments later the fog lit up with an eerie glow.

"Stephen! Stephen!"

Rain began to fall. Or maybe the fog was so thick it simply couldn't hold any more water in the air. Soft drops pattered around me. A shape, darker than the darkness, loomed above me. "Stephen!" I howled. The shape came at me.

"Jenny! I found you!" He was in my flashlight beam. Good, solid, wonderful, Stephen.

"We've got to get back to the castle!"

BOOM!!! Flash! Crackle! Flash! BOOM!

The world went white.

Then silent.

"KIDS WILL LOVE THIS FANTASY ADVENTURE THAT FEATURES LOTS OF ACTION AND A TOUCH OF ROMANCE. IT'S FAST-PACED, FUNNY, AND WARM. A REAL PAGE-TURNER!"
—**Page McBrier, author of**
the *Oliver and Company* series.

The Anywhere Ring

DON'T MISS THE FIRST BOOK
IN THIS EXCITING NEW SERIES!

MIRACLE ISLAND

Jenny was furious when her parents went off on
a tropical vacation without her and her little
brother. But when she discovered the
magical powers of her great-grandmother's ring, she learned that it
could take her anywhere
she wanted to go . . .

The Anywhere Ring series by Louise Ladd

MIRACLE ISLAND
CASTLE IN TIME

For Doug, who is everything to me.
With his wisdom, caring kindness, and love,
he has made it all possible.

My deep appreciation to Maurice Brick for his invaluable help with the Irish language, both Gaelic and modern.

And hugs and thanks also to Colleen Harrington, who cheerfully accompanied me through castles and countryside, and even praised my driving on the left-hand side of the road.

chapter one

I waited for Stephen in front of the statue in Piccadilly Circus, bouncing with happiness. Thanks to my beautiful, magical ring, I was in London, England! It was unbelievable, but true. I was actually here! I held my ring up to the streetlight, admiring the gold filigree setting and the deep red garnet stone. Now I was sure its magic could take me anywhere in the world.

Trying to spot Stephen, I looked up and down the streets. Piccadilly Circus seemed a silly name for a busy city intersection. There were no clowns or tents, only red double-decker buses and cars. Neon signs flashed ads and people strolled along the wet, crowded sidewalks. It was evening and I breathed in damp air and exhaust fumes.

"Jenny!" Stephen popped out of a cab that had pulled up at the curb.

The moment I saw him I went beyond happiness to pure heaven. His ears sort of stuck out like an elephant's, and he wasn't movie-star handsome, but he had a great laugh, a grin that lit up his face, and dark brown eyes that could turn melty-soft.

"You made it!" Stephen took both my hands in his. "You're really here! Your magic can take you to places other than the Caribbean!"

"Yes, isn't it super?" I'd met Stephen when the ring's magic took me to Miracle Island. He helped us out of a really humongous mess when my best friend, Carly, my little brother, Davy, and I got stuck there and couldn't get home. "Carly and I guessed the magic might work if I knew someone in London, or if I had a really deep-down desperate need to come. We're still not sure which it is, maybe both, but right now it doesn't matter, does it?"

"Not at all." He laughed, then held up my hand and gazed at the ring I'd inherited from my great-grandmother. The letter that came with it had said I must never tell any-one the secret or it would lose its power. Stephen and Carly had guessed that the magic came from the ring, but I'd never actually spoken the words.

"And it's not just London," I said. "I'm sure now that I can go anywhere in the world if it's important enough."

"And coming here was important? To see me?" He flashed that teasing grin.

I felt my cheeks turning pink. Stephen wasn't my boy-friend or anything like that. He was just a boy I'd met on Miracle. Okay, he'd kissed me a couple of times, and he said he liked me, but I still wasn't sure he thought I was . . . special. As in, *really* special.

"Uh, well, ummm . . ." I looked down at the wet sidewalk. "It's just that we never had a chance to say good-bye. We were zapped home to Connecticut while you were gone and . . ."

"I see." He tried to sound very serious. "You came all this way only to say an official good-bye?"

"Well . . . not exactly." By now my cheeks felt like they were flaming red. "I—I wanted to see you."

"That's good. I'm glad to see you too." His laugh rang out, startling the people passing by. "Come on, I'll take you home and introduce you to my family . . . or part of it." We started down the street. "My father and stepmother are expecting you. I told them you were a friend I met on vacation."

"I guess that's true enough." The only difference was I hadn't taken a plane to Miracle Island; my ring took me, in a sort of ragged way. But now I'd figured out most of the rules, so I shouldn't get into so much trouble again. I hoped.

After we'd been marooned in the Caribbean, we figured out that the only way to get back from one of our trips was to have someone I know call my name. Right now Carly was waiting back in Connecticut to bring me home.

Stephen led me toward a bus stop. "I think you'll like my sister, Margaret. She should be home soon. She's gone to meet a chap who rang up this afternoon. He said he was a distant cousin from America. He's stopping here on his way to Ireland."

"Ireland?" I said. "My parents plan to visit there sometime. My father's family came from County Cork a long time ago."

"We're part Irish too, on my mother's side," Stephen said, "and that's why this cousin, Patrick McSheehy, tracked us down. Our great-great-grandfathers were brothers, I think. I didn't get the story quite straight, but he said something about a family castle and buried treasure, so Margaret went dashing off to meet him."

"Buried treasure!"

"Not only treasure." Stephen shook his head. "There's also supposed to be an ancient curse on the McSheehy clan. Sounds a little wild to me, but Margaret became quite excited and insisted on seeing this chap. She tends to be a bit dramatic at times."

"I don't blame her," I said. "I think it's—"

"Why Jennifer Delaney, I didn't know you were in London!" a woman said behind me.

I whirled around. Mrs. Cummings, one of my mother's best friends, was standing not two feet away!

"Are you here with a school group?" Mrs. Cummings asked. "Your mother didn't say a word about it."

"I—I—I—" In this huge city with millions of people, why did my mother's friend have to spot *me*?

"You *are* Jenny Delaney, aren't you?" Mr. Cummings stood beside his wife. I hadn't noticed him at first.

His question gave me an idea. Imitating Stephen's British accent, I said, "I beg your pardon?"

"Come on, Jenny, I'd recognize you anywhere," Mrs. Cummings said. "What I can't understand is why your mother didn't tell me you'd be in London too. She knows we've been planning this trip for ages."

"I—I'm really quite sorry, madam," I said in my most exaggerated British. "I believe you've made a mistake. My name isn't Jenny. It's . . . McSheehy. Samantha Mc-Sheehy." It was the first thing that popped into my mind.

"Really?" Mrs. Cummings stepped back slightly and studied me. "But . . . I'm sure I recognize that blue skirt and sweater. You wore it when we all went out to dinner last spring."

Boy, Mrs. Cummings sure had a good memory! "I—I'm afraid I don't know what you're referring to."

I glanced at Stephen; he caught my desperate look.

Putting his arm around my shoulder, he said, "I'm terribly sorry, but you appear to have made a mistake. This is my sister, Samantha McSheehy. Apparently she bears quite a resemblance to your friend, but I can assure you she's not the person you take her for."

"Oh!" Mrs. Cummings said. "I'm really sorry. But I could have sworn . . ."

"Come along, Betsy," Mr. Cummings said. "Please excuse us," he told me. "Sorry to have bothered you." He began to lead his wife away.

"Oh, it was . . . no bother at all," I managed to say.

As they walked off I heard Mrs. Cummings muttering to him, "But, George, it's uncanny. She looks so much like Jenny. . . ."

I felt my knees go weak with relief. "Oh wow, Stephen, what a shock!"

"You were great. But remind me to give you a few tips on your British accent."

"Thanks a lot!" I whacked him on the arm. Lightly. "*I*

thought I sounded veddy, veddy English.'' Then I frowned a little. "I'm kind of sorry I had to fool Mrs. Cummings, though. She's a nice lady.''

"You had no choice, Jenny. You can't tell anyone about the . . . er''—he glanced at my ring—"magic, so how could you possibly explain?''

"I know, you're right.'' I glanced around at the crowded streets. "But . . . can we get out of here? I feel sort of . . . exposed.''

"Right. I thought I'd take you home by bus so we could sit on the upper deck and I could point out some of the London sights, but I'll hail a taxi instead.''

He raised his arm and signaled. A moment later one of the big black cabs pulled over and we jumped into the backseat. During the short drive Stephen showed me a few places like Hyde Park and Kensington Palace but I wasn't in much of a sight-seeing mood.

Besides the shock of running into Mrs. Cummings, I was suddenly nervous about meeting Stephen's father, Sir Richard. I'd never met a real live baronet before, but it wasn't just his title that scared me. Stephen had once let it slip out that his father sometimes advised the Queen of England on how to invest her money. I would be talking to a person who talked to Queen Elizabeth!

The taxi stopped in front of an elegant town house on a quiet side street. It was tall and narrow, five stories high, and looked something like the Bankses' house in *Mary Poppins,* a movie I used to watch on video when I was little. A cheerful lady opened the door and Stephen introduced me to Mrs. Leonard, the housekeeper.

As we walked down the hall I noticed paintings in gold frames, a thick Oriental carpet, and a number of doors opening off both sides. A mahogany staircase curved up to the second floor.

Stephen's father and his stepmother, Suzanne, were in the library, a comfortable room with tons of books and a crackling fire leaping up the chimney.

"Father, I'd like you to meet Jenny Delaney, my friend from Connecticut," Stephen said.

"Welcome to London, Miss Delaney." Sir Richard shook my hand. He was about the same height as Stephen, only a few inches taller than me, with the same slender but muscular build. His hair was sprinkled with gray and his eyes were blue instead of dark brown, but basically he was an older version of his son.

"Call me Jenny, please," I said, shaking the hand that shook the Queen's hand.

"Right, Jenny it is." He seemed to be a serious person, but when he smiled there was a sparkle in his eye. "And this is my wife, Suzanne."

Stephen's stepmother looked like she'd just stepped out of a magazine ad. Her dress was perfect, as if it would never dare wrinkle or get dirty, and her blond hair curved around her face in smooth waves.

"It's a pleasure to meet you, Jenny," she said. "Will you be able to join us for dinner?"

"Oh, thank you very much, but I can't stay long." I glanced at my watch. Carly would be calling me back in about fifteen minutes.

"Perhaps some other time then," Suzanne said.

The door flew open and a beautiful girl burst into the room, dragging a young man with copper-colored hair by the hand. "Papa, here's Pat, our long-lost cousin from America. He says we have a castle in Ireland, and there's a huge fortune in gold and jewels hidden somewhere in the mountains, and we're all going to be rich and famous when we find it!"

chapter two

"Margaret, where are your manners?" Suzanne said. "Would you kindly make proper introductions."

"Sorry." Stephen's sister didn't look the least bit sorry—she was bouncing with excitement. She wore jeans and a white sweater and her shiny reddish-brown hair fell around her shoulders like a cape. My first impression was that she was incredibly beautiful. Later, I realized she wasn't exactly pretty, but her gray-green eyes were so alive and her laugh was so bubbly that it hardly seemed to matter. Stephen had told me she was seventeen and wanted to be an actress. I could immediately see her starring in movies or on TV.

"Suzanne, Papa, may I present Mr. Patrick James McSheehy, from Queens, New York, in the United States."

Pat McSheehy was at least six feet tall and built like a bull. With his curly copper hair and blue-sky eyes, all he needed was a tweed cap and you'd think he'd stepped right off an Irish farm. I guessed he was about eighteen or nineteen, possibly twenty.

He stepped forward and shook Sir Richard's hand. "It's good to meet you, sir. I hope I'm not interrupting. Margaret insisted it would be all right."

"Of course. We're quite used to Meg's . . . er . . . enthusiasm," Sir Richard said. "This is my son, Stephen, and his friend Jennifer Delaney. She's also an American, from Connecticut."

"No kidding." Patrick winked at me. "We're practically neighbors."

"It looks like we've been invaded by the Yanks this evening," Sir Richard said with his dry smile. "And we thought we were rid of you lot after the Revolution, some two-hundred-odd years ago." He walked over to the fireplace and leaned against the mantel. "Did I understand Meg correctly? Are you a relative?"

"A very distant cousin." Patrick glanced at Suzanne, the second Mrs. Harrison. "On . . . well, Margaret's mother's side of the family."

Suzanne stiffened a bit, but her polite smile didn't fade a fraction. I guess it's not easy being a second wife when a relative of the first one drops by.

"I see," Sir Richard said. "I recall Claire mentioning a McSheehy grandparent somewhere in the past. I gather your relatives immigrated to America?"

"Yes, sir, during the potato famine, in the 1850s. But you know what they say about us Irish-Americans—we never forget the 'old country.' "

Mrs. Leonard, the housekeeper, knocked on the open

door. "Dinner is served, sir."

"Thank you," Sir Richard said. "Will you and Margaret join us, Mr. McSheehy?"

"Oh Papa, we couldn't eat another bite," Margaret said. "We stopped for fish and chips not an hour ago—we were utterly famished. You and Suzanne go ahead."

"If you're sure . . ." Suzanne moved quickly to the hallway and Sir Richard followed her out.

Margaret closed the door behind them, then settled herself on one end of the couch. "Pat, Jenny, do sit down and make yourselves comfortable. Stephen, wait until you hear Pat's story. We McSheehys really do have a castle on the west coast of Ireland. Of course, it doesn't actually belong to us anymore, and it's only a small castle in a remote part of the country, and it's in ruins, but who cares? Isn't it just too *too* romantic?"

"I suppose so," Stephen said, taking his father's place by the fire. "But what's all this about buried treasure?"

Pat sat on the other end of the couch and I perched on a chair across from them.

"I didn't say it was *buried* treasure, Stephen," Margaret said. "It may be buried, of course, but all we know is that our ancestor hid bags of gold and jewels in the mountains near the castle way back in the 1500s, when Queen Elizabeth the First's soldiers invaded the country."

"At least that's the family legend passed down over the years," Pat said. "A great-aunt and uncle went back to look for the treasure a long time ago but found nothing. Of course, they didn't get along too well, so possibly the curse kept the treasure hidden from them."

"What curse?" Stephen asked.

Margaret sighed with pleasure. "It's just so terribly Irish. I love it. You see, the king who hid the treasure was killed fighting the English. So was his faithful servant, so only the old grandmother knew exactly where the site was. Those were the only three who took the treasure up to the mountains." She paused for effect. "Except, there are two versions of the story. You tell them, Pat."

"Okay." He leaned forward. "One part of the family believes that two strangers went up into the mountains with them. If that's the case, those strangers could have easily returned later and stolen the jewels and gold, once the fighting was over. But most of the family insists the king would never take outsiders along on such a secret mission, so they say this version of the story can't be true."

"And the curse?" Stephen reminded them.

"I'm getting to it, Stephen," Margaret said. "You were always such an impatient little brother."

Stephen groaned. "And you were always such a bossy big sister. Can't you tell a simple story and leave out the dramatics?"

"What dramatics?" Margaret demanded with a theatrical wave of her arm.

Pat chuckled. "I'll tell the story, then."

"Please, could you?" I said, glancing at my watch. Carly would be calling me back to Connecticut very soon. "I can't stay much longer and I'm dying to hear it."

"I'd forgotten about your . . . appointment, Jenny," Stephen said. "How much longer do you have?"

"Just a few minutes. What about the curse?"

"Well . . ." Margaret paused for effect again, then glanced at Stephen and me and hurried on. "After the king was killed, the rest of the family fought over who was going to be the heir. There was a teenage son, but also several brothers, and they all wanted to become the new lord of the castle—and own the treasure, of course. The arguments went on and on, until finally the old grandmother was completely fed up with them all."

"You see," Pat added, "she was also a powerful witch, and back in those days they really believed in magic."

"That's right." Margaret nodded. Stephen and I glanced at each other. We knew about magic. "So she cast a curse and said that the treasure would remain hidden 'until those seeking it came in peace and harmony.' Only then would the secret be revealed."

"And knowing the McSheehys the way I do," Pat said, "I'm not surprised that it hasn't been found over the last four hundred years. The McSheehys are great fighters, one and all, as you two just demonstrated a moment ago." He grinned at Stephen and Margaret.

Stephen looked sheepish. "Don't pay any attention to us. I'm always teasing Meggie."

"That's right," she agreed. "He's been a pest ever since he was in nappies. See? There's something we agree upon!"

Stephen reached down and yanked a lock of Margaret's long hair. She squealed and swatted his hand away.

I burst out laughing. Stephen and Margaret reminded me of myself and my six-year-old brother, Davy. I guess big sisters and little brothers are the same everywhere.

Pat studied Margaret, as if trying to make up his mind about something. After a moment he pulled a postcard out of his pocket.

"There's one other part of the story I haven't told you yet, Margaret," he said.

"What?" She pushed Stephen away and stared at Pat, fascinated.

He handed her the postcard. "This is a picture of the oldest harp known in Ireland. It's in a glass case at Trinity College in Dublin. As you may know, the harp is one of Ireland's most famous symbols. Poets, called *filí*, used to tell stories with their songs. Along with the *seanchaís*— who were sort of traveling bards of a lesser class—they became the keepers of history and legends through their music."

"I didn't know that," Margaret said.

"I did," Stephen said. "One of my favorite instructors is Irish and last year he offered a seminar in the Irish language, Gaelic. I took the course and learned a few words, and a bit about the country as well. If you want to be a true McSheehy, Margaret, you should do the same, instead of wasting your time with acting and singing lessons."

She began to react to his teasing, then decided to ignore him. Tossing her head, she asked Pat, "How is the harp connected with the story?"

"To me, the harp *is* the story," Pat said. "I'm a musician. I play a number of instruments, but I love the Irish harp the best. And the McSheehy grandmother owned an ancient harp at the time of the English invasion. It was given to her by a famous *file* after her herbs cured him of a serious illness. She became his student, which was most unusual for a woman, and it's said that when she played, the angels sang. She loved that harp, so along with the gold and jewels, it was hidden in the mountains to keep it from the English.''

"It was?'' Margaret asked. "Do you think it's survived all these years?''

"I don't know. I hope so, because if it has, it will be older than the oldest known harp in Ireland.''

"Wow,'' I said quietly. Pat was so serious about this we were all a little awed. "It would be very valuable, then, wouldn't it?''

"It would be beyond price, especially to me.'' He shrugged and half grinned. "Of course, I'd also like to prove to all the McSheehys back home that the old family legend is really true.''

"It's too bad Mum isn't here,'' Margaret said. "She might know more about it.''

"Could we call her?'' Pat asked.

"I'm afraid not,'' Stephen said. "She's somewhere in India on a mission for UNICEF. She phones once in a while, but there's no way to reach her, since she moves around so much.''

"We could leave a message,'' Margaret said, "but unless it's an emergency, it might be a week before she gets back to us.''

"I'll probably be gone by then,'' Pat said. "I'm flying to Ireland Thursday morning. What about her parents or other relatives?''

"All of them died a long time ago, before Margaret and I were born," Stephen said.

"Wait a moment!" Margaret jumped up and ran over to the bookcase. "Somewhere in here is Mum's old scrapbook." She opened a lower cabinet door and began to rummage around. "I remember her showing me pictures one time when I was little, and I think there just might have been a castle."

Stephen went to help her look and I checked my watch. Time was running out. They finally hauled out a large leather-bound volume. We all gathered around the couch while Margaret flipped through photographs of babies and dogs, picnics and sleigh rides, horses and carriages.

"Here it is!" Margaret pointed to a page of country shots. The original black-and-white photo had faded to brown and gold but standing up in a field with high, rocky mountains behind it were the tumbledown ruins of a castle.

"Nineteen twenty-one." She squinted at the handwriting. "D-u-n-s-l-i-a-b-h. It must be Gaelic. I don't even know how to pronounce it."

"*Dunsliabh*, Dune-slee-av," Stephen said. "*Dun* means 'fort' and *sliabh* is 'hill,' I think. I may be wrong, though; it's been a while since I took that course."

"Hill-fort," Pat said.

"Why is it in ruins?" I asked.

"It was sacked during one of the invasions," Pat said. "The McSheehys lost their power over the years, partly thanks to the English taking over the country, and partly because they fought so much among themselves. My branch of the McSheehys became farmers and the potato famine wiped them out, along with the rest of the country.''

"I know about the famine. Thousands and thousands died. It was horrible," Margaret said.

"You should hear the stories," Pat said. "We Mc-Sheehys have sure kept up the *file* tradition. My grandfather tells it as if all the misery and tragedy of the famine happened to him personally, even though he was born a long time afterward in the United States.''

Margaret gazed at the photo of the castle, then suddenly sat up straight. "I've decided. I'm going to Ireland with you, Pat. I want to see this castle for myself. Do you mind if I tag along?''

"Of course not. I'd love to have company.'' From the way he looked at Margaret, I could see he was especially interested in *her* company.

"And we *are* compatible, aren't we?" Margaret said. "In case the old grandmother's curse is still in effect, we'll be searching in harmony, won't we?''

"Yes, great harmony . . .'' Pat agreed. "Cousins united in peace . . .''

"Just a moment, Meggie," Stephen said. "You can't go flying off to Ireland. You have school and you know Father would never allow you to cut classes.''

She stuck her tongue out at him. "That shows how much you know. I don't have any classes, only exams, and mine aren't scheduled until the end of next week. I'd only have to miss school Thursday and Friday—and Papa won't even know about it, unless a certain big-mouth baby brother rats on me.''

"I say, Margaret, that's terribly unfair.'' Stephen jumped

up and strode across the room. "You're asking me to lie for you."

"Not lie," she said happily. "Just don't tell."

My head began to ache. Carly was calling me back to Connecticut. Talk about rotten timing!

"Stephen," I said, standing up. "I hate to leave, but I *have* to go."

"What?" He gave me a blank look for a moment, his mind on his sister. "Oh! Right. I'll see you to the door."

"Stephen," Margaret said. "Are you sending Jenny off on her own? That's not very polite of you."

"It's okay," I said quickly. My head was really beginning to pound. "I have a friend waiting. Sorry, Stephen, but can we hurry?"

He raced to the library door and yanked it open. I said a fast good-bye and ran down the hall after him, crossing my fingers that no one was around. The last thing I wanted was for Sir Richard to see me vanish into thin air.

"The coast is clear," Stephen reported, reaching into the closet. "Here's your bag that you left behind on Miracle Island." He handed me the beach bag, then fumbled in his jacket pocket, searching for something. "When will you be back?"

"I don't know. Soon, I hope." I almost moaned out loud, my head hurt so much.

"Take this to use for the magic next time. It's a photo of this house. Instead of going to Piccadilly, you can come directly here."

"Thanks. I—"

*   *   *

London vanished and I found myself in Carly's room, sitting on her bed, exactly where I'd been when I left an hour and a half before.

She flashed me her cheerful freckle-faced grin. "I guess our experiment worked, huh? You went to London!"

"I sure did." I held my throbbing head with both hands, although the ache was already starting to fade. "Wow, Carly, I have so much to tell you I don't know where to start. But one thing's for sure—I've got to get back to London and find out what happens with Margaret and Pat and the treasure and the castle!"

chapter three

"*Treasure? Castle?* What castle?" Carly asked. "And who are Pat and Margaret? Do you mean Stephen's sister?"

"Yes, but it's a long story, and I'd better leave right now or I'll be late for dinner and Miss Cuddy will be mad." Miss Cuddy was a dragon lady who was staying with Davy and me while our parents were on vacation.

"Come on, Jenny," she begged as I stood up. "Hey, you brought back the beach bag!"

"Yeah, I'll go through it later and give you your stuff. I've got to hurry now." I headed for the door. "I'll call you tonight and tell you everything."

"What?" Carly squealed, coming after me. "Is that any way to treat a person who sat here for an hour and a half with the creepy ghost you left behind, while you're off to castles in England?"

"Ireland, not England," I said. "And I haven't seen a castle, except in a picture. Was my ghost really creepy?"

Whenever we traveled with the ring, we left behind shadowy-type shapes that Davy called ghosts. I'd never seen one because I'd never stayed behind.

Carly followed me to the door. "Yes, it was totally weird, and from now on you're leaving from the closet so I don't have to stare at it. And you're not going to London again, unless you sit down and tell me everything right now!"

"But Miss Cuddy . . ." I looked at my watch, then my best friend's face. "Oh, why not? Let her yell at me if she wants. My parents will be home in a couple of days anyway."

"Tell all!" Carly, grinning, led me to her bed.

I plopped down and told her the whole story. Stephen's family, Pat, the castle in Ireland, the lost treasure, and the curse. "But the curse won't be a problem if Margaret goes with Pat, because even if they're both McSheehys, they like each other," I finished.

Carly sighed with happiness. "It's all so romantic. I can't wait to find out what happens."

"Me too." I looked at my watch. "Eeek! I'm super-late." I ran for the door. "Gotta go. I'll call you later."

My little brother, Davy, threw himself on me the moment I got home, complaining about Miss Cuddy. Then, during supper, *she* complained about *him*. That was after she bawled me out for being late. She'd already earned the title of World's Worst Baby-sitter and I was glad my parents would—finally—be back soon.

As soon as I put Davy to bed, Miss Cuddy curled up

with her true love, the TV, and I called Carly. We made plans for the next day.

My hopes were doomed. During homeroom Tuesday morning they announced the basketball game against West-port that was canceled because of a snowstorm in January had been rescheduled for that afternoon. I had to go be-cause the team counted on me.

I'm not a great player, but I'm the tallest girl on the team—sometimes I think I'm the tallest girl in the world—so I usually end up making my share of the baskets. I boarded the bus, thinking about Stephen and Margaret, and Pat's castle. I should have stayed home. I missed three free throws and we lost the game by a truly embarrassing score.

On Wednesday, Mom and Dad came back from the Car-ibbean. They arrived, tanned and happy, shortly after school was out. I had my hands full with Davy, trying to keep him from blurting out the truth about our magical trips to Miracle Island. A combination of dark threats featuring unspeakable torture, and sixteen zillion promises to take him back to Miracle as soon as possible, kept his mouth shut, but I didn't dare leave him alone with our parents for a second. I was totally wiped by the time he finally went to bed.

The best part about the day was waving good-bye to Miss Cuddy. *That* was a real pleasure.

At last, *at last,* AT LAST it was Thursday afternoon. Davy was invited to his friend Brian Moore's house, so I wouldn't have to stand guard over him. He could tell Brian anything he wanted and Mrs. Moore would assume it was a game of pretend. She was used to the two of them flying to the moon and capturing dinosaurs in the backyard.

Carly and I walked—actually we almost ran—home from school together. She was as impatient as I was to find out what had happened in London while I was gone. Her parents wouldn't be back from work until at least six o'clock and her older brothers were always out somewhere, doing something, so we had her house to ourselves.

Carly took off her ski jacket, but I left mine on. It was February and London was just as cold as it was here in Connecticut.

As soon as we got to her room, Carly opened her closet door. "And heeeeere it is!" she sang out like the ringmaster at the circus.

"Are you serious?" I asked. "You *really* want me to sit in your smelly old closet?"

"It's not too smelly," she said. "Look, I even made room for you."

It was a big closet and she'd piled all her junk on the sides, so there was a space for me to sit in the middle without touching anything. "You've gotta be kidding," I said.

"Nope. What do you care anyway? You won't be here to notice." She shook her head and her red-Brillo curls bounced like tiny springs. "You'll be gone three hours and I'm not gonna spend all that time staring at a yucky ghost."

"Is it really that gross?" I asked.

"Major gross," she said. "Besides, it's safer this way, in case one of my brothers comes home or something."

"You've got a point." I ducked under Carly's skirts and

dresses and sat down, scrunching myself in between shoes, ice skates, camping gear, library books, and a ton of other junk. "What are you going to do while I'm gone?"

"My homework. Get it over with. *Back to the Future, Part 99* is on cable tonight and I want to watch it." She stood there, her blue eyes wistful. "You're so lucky, Jenny. I wish I could go to England too."

"Yeah, I know." I felt guilty for a moment because I was the lucky owner of the ring and she wasn't. "But you're the only one who can call me back. I can't trust anyone except you."

"Good old reliable Carly." She pushed out a laugh.

"I'll tell you all about it." Like that could make up for missing out on the fun.

"Say hi to Stephen for me." She watched me pull the photo of the London town house out my pocket, then slowly closed the closet door, leaving only a crack of light to spill in. I played with my ring and concentrated on the picture.

I stood on the sidewalk across the street from Stephen's house, shivering in the cold sun. A mailman almost ran into me. Fortunately he'd been looking down, shuffling letters in his bag, when I appeared out of nowhere. Still, he was surprised. I nodded as if I had every right to be there, then crossed the street and rang Stephen's doorbell.

Mrs. Leonard let me in. "Good afternoon, miss."

That answered one of my questions. I wasn't sure what time of day I'd arrive. I'd land whenever the photo Stephen gave me had originally been taken. The first time I went to

Miracle, it was nighttime in Connecticut, but I appeared on the beach around eleven the next morning, since the photo I'd used was taken at that time of day.

"Is Stephen here?" I asked politely.

"He's in the library with Mrs. Harrison, having tea." Mrs. Leonard took my jacket, then led me down the hall, past several open doors. I noticed that the house was even nicer than I remembered, with high ceilings, plush rugs, and antique furniture. In the library, sunlight streamed through the windows, sparkling on a silver tea service set on a table beside Stephen's stepmother, Suzanne.

"Jenny!" Stephen jumped up the moment he saw me. "I was wondering when I'd see you again."

Suzanne picked up the silver teapot. "Hello, Jenny. Will you join us for tea?"

"Um, sure . . . I mean, yes, thank you." I perched on the edge of the chair Stephen led me to. "I hope you don't mind that I just dropped in. I'm sorry I didn't call. . . ."

"It's all right," Stephen said quickly. "You came at a good time. We're expecting Margaret to ring up any minute. She flew to Ireland with Pat early this morning. They're renting a car and driving to the coast to search for the McSheehy castle."

"So she went after all," I said. "I wondered if—"

"We found a note from her this morning." Stephen glanced at his stepmother. "My father is in France on business. He doesn't know she's gone yet, and Suzanne has agreed we don't need to upset him, if Margaret keeps her promise to call us by teatime."

"I must say, I quite disapprove of Margaret running off like this." Suzanne handed me a delicate cup decorated with violets. It was so fragile I was afraid to touch it. "But her father is handling a difficult negotiation today and I see no sense in worrying him yet. Will you have some cream cake, my dear?"

I had the cake, several hot buttery scones, and a delicious, gooey puddinglike thing called trifle while we waited to hear from Margaret. Suzanne asked me about my family and I told her Dad taught English in high school and my mother was a computer consultant.

We talked about this and that, then talked some more.

Finally the teapot was empty and only crumbs were left on the plates. Still Margaret didn't call.

Suzanne stood up. "Really, it's quite annoying. Your father will not be pleased that your sister has broken her promise."

"I'm sure she has a good reason." Stephen looked worried. "She always keeps her word, you know she does. Maybe their car broke down."

"Surely she could have reached a telephone by now." Suzanne went to the door. "When I speak to your father later this evening I will tell him about her irresponsible behavior."

After she left, Stephen closed the door and began to pace around the room. "Margaret is *not* irresponsible. I know she seems rather headstrong and overly dramatic at times, but if she makes a promise, she keeps it. Even if the castle is in a remote area, there should be a village with a telephone nearby. Something has gone wrong."

"I'm sure she's okay," I said, although I wasn't sure at all. "Maybe there was plane trouble and her flight was delayed."

"Good thought. I'll check." Stephen called Shannon Airport. The flight had landed on time. Then he talked to the car-rental people. Yes, Pat and Margaret had picked up their car. No, no breakdowns reported.

Finally Stephen called the police and hospitals in the area. No accidents, no trouble anywhere concerning an American boy and an English girl.

Margaret and Pat had simply vanished into the Irish countryside.

"It's all my fault." Stephen began to pace again, stalking back and forth in front of the fire. "If I'd told my father what she was planning, this wouldn't have happened. She'd still be safe at home. How could I let her do this?"

I noticed that he kept rubbing his hands together as if they bothered him. Suddenly he stopped and stared at his palms.

"Margaret's in trouble," he announced. "She needs help."

"I know, but—"

"Jenny, she's in serious trouble. Look." He held his hands out to me. The palms were bright red. "This has only happened twice before, once when she broke her leg at school and once when she was thrown from a horse and knocked unconscious. Both times I was miles away, and both times my hands began to burn and itch."

"Wow, that's awesome," I said. "Although I've read about things like that happening between twins. I guess you two are really close, aren't you?''

"Yes, we are." He was very serious. "Jenny, you have to take me to the castle."

"But . . . I'm not sure I can," I said. "I've never tried to go anywhere with the magic, except from home. Can I go from England to Ireland? I don't know if it works that way."

"Then let's find out." He took the leather scrapbook out of the cupboard. Together we quickly flipped through the pages.

The picture of the castle was missing. The little black triangles that held the corners of the photo framed only a faded black square on the page. Margaret must have taken it with her. Next to it was a photo showing fields and stone walls, with mountains in the distance.

"Is this the same place?" I asked. "Do those mountains look like the others?"

"I think so," Stephen said. "But I can't be sure. We'll have to hope they are." He slipped the photo out of the scrapbook and gave it to me. "Jenny, please."

I glanced around the library. "We can't try from here. Remember the ghosts Davy said we left behind when I took you back to Miracle Island? I know my ghost is in Connecticut because Carly saw it, but you'd leave yours here, since it's your home. Is there a private place where no one will stumble over it?"

"Come on." He took my hand and dragged me down the hall. As we started up the staircase I spotted my jacket on the coatrack near the front door.

"Whoa," I called. "I'll bet it's cold in Ireland. Let's go prepared, if we *can* go."

"You're right." Stephen came back down the stairs and dug his own coat out of the closet, then asked, "Now are you ready?"

When I nodded he led the way up to the attic floor of the town house. Something nagged at me—we should be doing something else to prepare, in case this experiment worked—but he was so impatient to find Margaret, I didn't have time to think what it was.

On the top floor Stephen opened the door to a small room filled with broken chairs, rolled-up rugs, and boxes of odds and ends.

"This used to be one of the servants' rooms," he said. "We hardly ever come up here anymore. It's a safe place to leave a ghost."

He closed the door, pushed a rickety table out of the way, and made a spot for us to sit on the floor.

"I'm not sure this will work, Stephen," I said, trying to remember all the rules of the magic. At least we definitely had a desperate urgency to go to Ireland. "And if it does, we may not end up anywhere near the castle, if this is the wrong picture."

"Jenny, think positive." His grin flashed for a moment. "You can do it."

Stephen has the greatest grin in the world. It's almost impossible to resist.

"Okay," I said. "Here we come, Ireland. I hope."

We sat facing each other, our knees making contact. Anyone touching me comes along on my trips. I spread my jacket over my lap to hide my hands while I played with the garnet ring. I concentrated on the picture, wishing to be there. I thought of Margaret and Pat, maybe up in those mountains, maybe in trouble, maybe desperately needing us. I concentrated hard, imagining us in that field, facing those rocky, steep rugged mountains.

An icy wind blew through my sweater. We were sitting on green grass. I saw rough rocks, soft white woolly shapes. Sheep! Sheep everywhere, and a few cows too. I could smell them, that distinct farm odor coming in whiffs as the strong wind blew freezing against my cheeks.

"You did it, Jenny," Stephen said, helping me stand up.

The sky above us was absolutely huge, lead gray with heavy clouds. Beyond the farthest fields the mountains rose up in steep giant humps that disappeared into thick fog.

"Are we near the castle?" Holding my breath, I turned around.

The ruined castle loomed behind us, its stone walls crumbling but still radiating a sense of eerie power. The remains of the square central tower poked into the dull sky, broken and jagged. Smaller round towers clung to it on either side and crumbling walls swung out and away, melting into rock piles where sheep grazed on coarse weeds.

Beyond the castle, an enormous valley dropped away, flowing down and down into the distance, where it finally met the sea. The valley was laced with stone walls marking off fields, and a small village huddled in the center. The sun was low, turning the far-off ocean into a glittering sheet of liquid gold.

"Look, Jenny." Stephen pointed to the right. A small black sedan was parked by the castle wall. "You can tell by the decal on the window that it's a rental car."

The car was empty. The entire countryside was empty, except for the sheep and cows. The clouds thickened. The sky grew darker and darker.

I shivered.

"Put your jacket on, Jenny," Stephen said. He'd already slipped into his and now he helped me into mine. Hands shaking, I fumbled with the zipper.

A shrill whistle sounded from the castle. Suddenly an animal shot out of an opening at the base of the tower and ran straight at us!

chapter four

The animal, a black-and-white sheepdog, rushed toward us, then flashed past, headed for a group of fat cows.

My heart, which had jumped into my throat, slowly settled into its normal place.

The shrill whistling continued from the castle and the dog responded to each change in tone. Yipping and darting around the cows' hooves, it drove half a dozen of them into a small group. Once they were rounded up, the dog herded them over to the castle wall. The whistles stopped and the dog, quiet now, circled the cows until they calmed down and began to graze.

"That dog is a genius," I said.

"Quite remarkable," Stephen agreed.

The sky had grown almost black. Now it suddenly burst open, dumping buckets of rain on us.

Stephen grabbed my hand. "Let's go, Jenny!"

"Where?" I didn't move.

"The castle—shelter!"

"We don't know who's in there!" I dug my feet into the ground.

"Obviously the dog's owner."

"Yes, but who is he?"

A voice shouted, but it was hard to hear over the roar of the rain. I spotted a carrot-colored mop of hair poking out from the ruins. For a second I thought it was Carly—she has the same flame-orange curls. Then I realized it was a boy, maybe nine or ten years old.

"What's he saying?" I couldn't understand a word.

Stephen laughed. "He says we're 'eejits' and why don't we come in out of the wet?"

The dog, tail wagging, trotted over to its master. The two disappeared inside the stone tower.

"Come on." Stephen started off and I hurried to keep up with him. We crossed a low basin that circled the castle—I guess it used to be the moat—and stepped up to the gaping hole that was the main entrance.

The opening ran under the square tower and formed a short tunnel. At both ends, plastic sheets hung down, weighted with stones to keep them from blowing in the wind.

The boy and dog sat next to a small fire that sent up swirls of blue smoke. A battered kettle chirped on a bed of hot stones and several cans and boxes were scattered among a collection of tattered pillows.

It was toasty warm, although the air was rather smoky. I held my hands over the fire, glad to be out of the rain, and said, "Thanks for inviting us in."

"Sure and it's eejits ye be," the boy said, with a grin as wide as the Irish sky. "Are ye simple?" His thick accent was musical, but it wasn't easy to understand him.

"Probably." Stephen's hair was plastered to his head, making his large ears stick out more than usual. "We're looking for two people. We think that's their car outside. Have you seen anyone nearby?"

The boy studied us for a moment. He was young, but smart enough to be cautious with strangers. Finally he asked, "And who might ye be?"

"We're . . . er . . . visitors," Stephen said. "Looking for my sister and her friend."

He gave us another careful look, then found a rag and began to dry the dog's coat. "Where'd ye come from?"

I knew he was asking how we suddenly appeared in his fields, but I decided to misunderstand him. "I'm from America, although my family came from Ireland a long time ago. My name is Jenny Delaney, and this is Stephen Harrison."

"America? I've got an uncle over there. Boston, it is." His bright, sea-blue eyes lit up. "Do ye know him? Mickey O'Reilly? Him's got the same name as me."

"I don't think I've met him." I knew Stephen was impatient to find Margaret, but maybe it wasn't polite to ask questions right away. Kneeling down by the fire, I said, "So you're Mickey. You've got a beautiful dog. May I pet him?"

"*Her.* She's Molly. She's a good 'un." Mickey rubbed her ears.

"She's really smart." I held my hand out for her to

smell, then stroked her thick coat. She looked like a collie but was much smaller, with a blunter nose.

"I trained her meself," Mickey boasted. "Wi' me da's help, a' course," he added to be truthful.

Stephen had walked over to the end of the tunnel and was peering around the plastic. "Jenny, come look."

I joined him. Several ancient stone cottages lined the courtyard, all roofless. The rain poured down inside the walls and blew in through the empty windows. "They'll be ruined. Why doesn't the owner fix the roofs?"

"It's the duty," Mickey said. "Take off the roof and ye have no duty to pay."

"Duty means taxes," Stephen translated for me. "Does your family own this place?" he asked Mickey.

"Sure, they don't." He poked up the fire. I noticed he wasn't burning wood but something that looked like black-ish-brown bricks. "Do I look like a millionaire?" He chuckled and pointed to his soot-stained jacket. "Me da rents the land for the grazin' from a Dublin gent."

"Is the landlord named McSheehy?" Stephen asked.

"He's not. The McSheehys're long gone from here. Done in by the troubles they were, and left with not two-pence to rub together."

Mickey was a little more relaxed now, so I said casually, "We're looking for Stephen's sister and her cousin, a guy named Pat McSheehy. Have you seen them?"

"Might have." He seemed to have decided he could trust us. "There was two headed for the mountains when me and Molly got here. Packs they had on their backs, though who would want to be campin' in the middle a' winter I don't know. The mountains can be fierce if the weather turns bad.''

I looked out at the icy rain drenching the fields. ''You mean it gets worse than this?''

''Why, 'tis only a soft day now, down here.'' He winked, then pointed to the mountain humps that disappeared into the fog. ''Up there, who's to know?''

''Didn't you warn them not to go up?'' Stephen asked.

''Why now, 'twasn't my business, was it?'' He added another brown lump to the fire. ''Anyway, they were up the way a bit, and I knew well they wouldn't hear me.''

''We've got to go find them, Jenny.'' Stephen began to zip up his jacket.

''Now?'' I asked. ''We won't be able to see anything.''

''She's right, ye know,'' Mickey said. ''Bide a bit. The wet'll blow past soon. What's the sense in four of ye lost up there?''

''He's right, Stephen,'' I said. ''Let's wait a little while.''

Frustrated, Stephen slowly unzipped his jacket, staring out at the rain and fog.

Mickey offered us tea, but he had only one tin mug, so we said thanks anyway. He measured a few loose tea leaves out of a metal canister, poured in boiling water, then added milk from a small bottle.

Trying not to worry about Margaret and Pat up in the mountains, I kept asking Mickey questions. I found out he lived down in the valley, and his father sent him up here once in a while to check on the animals. He'd fixed up this shelter so he could wait out the storms that often blew in from the ocean. Today he and Molly would be taking the cows that were expecting calves down to a field closer to home.

I kept watching the fire, wondering how those brown bricks could burn. Finally I asked Mickey the secret.

"Why, 'tis peat. From the bogs," he added when I looked blank.

Stephen had been pacing up and down the short tunnel, but he stopped to explain to me, "Bogs are like swamps, filled with dead plants and trees that have built up for hundreds of years. Ireland is full of bogs and peat makes good fuel. All you have to do is cut it, dry it, and burn it."

"*All!*" Mickey snorted, pretending to be insulted. "It's sure and *ye've* never swung a *sleánn* in your life."

"You're right," Stephen said with a wry smile. "I'm sure it's hard work."

Mickey nodded wisely. "Sure and it is. Come back in the spring and me da and I will show the *Sasanach* a peat bog."

"*Sasanach,*" Stephen repeated. "I suppose it's obvious, then, that I'm British?"

"Sure and it's written all over ye," Mickey said.

"Look," I said. "The rain has stopped."

It was amazing how fast the clouds cleared away. Within a few minutes the fog had lifted and we could see the mountains rising up steep and rocky above us. Some of the highest peaks were streaked with snow.

Mickey put out his fire and whistled instructions to Molly. As she began to herd the cows toward the valley, he said, "I'm off home now. Good luck to ye." He set out on the long walk down.

Stephen had gone over to check out the car. It wasn't locked and I could see him looking in the glove compartment. "Here's the rental agreement," he called to me. "It's signed by Pat, so that confirms it. They've got to be up in those mountains somewhere. Let's get going."

"Yeah, we'd better hurry," I said. "Look how low the sun is. It'll be setting soon. Why didn't we think to bring flashlights?" I checked my watch. "Oh no!"

"What's the matter?"

"Carly will be calling me home in just a few minutes! I didn't realize how late it is." Then one of the problems that had been nagging at me before we left London hit me smack in the face. "Now I know what we forgot! We didn't make plans to get *you* back home."

"I'm not going until I find Margaret, so it doesn't matter." He started off toward the mountain.

I ran to catch up with him. "But, Stephen, I don't have much time. You'll have to come to the States with me, then I'll take you back to England. Carly won't mind waiting while we make one extra short trip."

"I'm not leaving until I find my sister." He kept walking at a fast pace.

"If you think I'm going to leave you here alone, you're crazy!" I was trotting to keep up with him. "We left so fast, we don't have anything! No flashlights, no camping equipment, no food—"

"Mickey said both Pat and Margaret wore backpacks, so

they must have supplies. I'll be fine as soon as I catch up with them.''

"But that could take all night! There's no way I'm leaving you alone up in those mountains. Another storm could hit anytime." I grabbed his arm, trying to slow him down. "Stephen, please be reasonable."

He stopped walking and pried my fingers off his jacket. "Look, this is all my fault. I should have told my father what Margaret was planning to do. Now she's in trouble and I'm here to help her. *You're* the crazy one if you think I'm going to jump back to the safety of home and leave her and Pat out in the wilderness." He started off again at a fast pace.

I hurried to catch up. He was so stubborn! How could I get through to him? "Like you just said, Pat is with her. He's big and strong. I'm sure he'll take care of her."

"What if he can't? What if he's hurt, or even dead?"

I shivered at the thought.

"I don't mean to scare you, Jenny," Stephen said. "But this is serious. I know my sister. Margaret would have called as she promised unless something went terribly wrong."

"But how can you help them if you get hurt too? I can't leave you here alone!"

"We made a terrible mistake rushing off unprepared the way we did." Stephen's eyes were bleak. "I take full blame for that too. But I'm here now and I'm going to do whatever it takes to find her."

My head began to ache. "Carly's calling me. Stephen, I

have to go and you have to come with me. I'll bring you back here as soon as I can."

"You know that will be hours from now. That's the way the magic works. In those two hours I'm sure I can find Margaret."

"Please come with me." I grabbed his jacket and hung on tight. If I was touching him, he'd have to come with me.

He tore my hands away and began to run. "I'll leave you a message," he shouted. "Over there!" He pointed to a rock wall at the edge of the field.

I dashed after him, almost blind from the throbbing in my head.

He raced across the field, scattering frightened sheep. "Bring a flashlight!"

"Stephen!" I screamed.

"Hush." Carly put her hand over my mouth. "My brother just came home. Don't yell like that or he'll be in here to find out what's going on."

"Oh no!" I gasped. "I'm back! And Stephen isn't!"

chapter five

"Take it easy, Jenny." Carly took her hand off my mouth. "Keep your voice down or my brother will hear you."

"I left Stephen . . . alone in the mountains!" I gasped, out of breath from chasing him across the fields. "I didn't want to . . . but he's so stubborn—"

"Come out of the closet and tell me what happened," she said.

I crawled out from under her clothes and staggered to my feet, "He wouldn't . . . listen to me! He's such . . . an idiot! I tried . . . to grab him, but . . . he got away from me."

"What are you *talking* about?" Carly demanded. "Sit down on my bed and catch your breath."

"There isn't time. . . . I've got to go . . . back for him right away!"

Carly led me to her bed and I collapsed on it.

"Calm down, Jenny, and listen." She stood over me, her arms folded. "You know as well as I do that no matter when you leave here, you'll get back there three hours after you first arrived. That's the way the magic works, so you don't have to rush back right now."

She was right. I relaxed slightly.

"You're a mess," she said.

She was right about that too. My sneakers and jeans were muddy, my jacket soaked, my hair falling in my face.

"You can't go home looking like that." Carly began to dig around in her drawers. "You left a pair of jeans here the last time you slept over. Where did I put them? I'll loan you a sweater, but you'll have to scrape the mud off your shoes—mine would never fit you. . . ."

Somehow her fussing and the simple business of getting cleaned up helped me calm down. I told her everything that had happened. "I feel so awful! Here I am, warm and dry and safe, and Stephen and Margaret and Pat are wandering around on an Irish mountain, cold and wet, and maybe hurt too."

"Don't get all worked up again," Carly said. "You've got to stay cool or you won't be able to help them. Let's make a list of what you should take with you."

Carly and her lists! She was a nut about them, but I have to admit it helped to see our plans written down in black and white. I'd take a backpack stuffed with a change of clothes for everyone, plus a carton of granola bars and a warm blanket. I'd never be able to carry four sleeping bags, so we settled on one, for whoever needed it most. Carly's family went camping a lot, so she had a complete first-aid kit and a super-heavy-duty flashlight.

"I don't think you can carry any more than that," she decided. "Not up a mountainside."

"Gosh, Carly, what if I can't find them?"

"Before you worry about that, let's figure out how you're going to get back to Ireland. It's a school night. Do you think your mom will let you come over here anyway?"

"Only if it has to do with schoolwork." Carly and I were in different classes, and we had different homework assignments. I thought a moment. "I know! The science fair! Don't you think it's about time we got to work on our project?"

"Excellent. And our project is . . . ?"

"The mountains of Europe—especially Ireland!" I left, promising I'd be back right after dinner.

Carly had a way of cheering me up, but at home I kept thinking of Stephen and the magic. Mom had made barbecued chicken and mashed potatoes, but all I tasted was sawdust.

At least I'd solved the problem about Davy and our secret trips to Miracle Island. That morning I'd told Mom that while they were on vacation, Davy and I played a game every day. We pretended we had gone to the Caribbean too, and I made up all kinds of stories about our adventures to keep him entertained. The problem was, now Davy thought he'd really gone to the island. So, if he started talking like he'd been there, she'd understand, wouldn't she? Mom said she would. I felt a little guilty, but what could I do? I couldn't tell her about the magic ring.

Now, tonight, when I asked if I could work on our science project at Carly's house, Dad got excited.

"That's a great idea, honey, European mountains," Dad said. "The Alps, the Pyrenees . . . you could demonstrate how they were formed, but you could also talk about their history. Did you know Hannibal tried to cross the Alps on elephants? Then there are the Scottish highlands and Bonnie Prince Charlie. . . . And did you read the article about the man they found preserved in ice near the Italian border? He was thousands of years old. . . ."

Dad went on, brimming with ideas. To make myself feel less guilty, I vowed that Carly and I would actually do the project for the science fair. As soon as Stephen and Margaret and Pat were safely home.

Even though I knew that no matter when I left Connecticut, I'd arrive back at the castle only three hours later than I first arrived—and there was nothing I could change to speed that up—dinner dragged on as I pictured Stephen wandering around alone on the mountain, Margaret, or Pat, hurt, trapped in a storm. . . .

"Jenny, did you hear me?" Mom asked.

"I'm sorry." I shook my head to clear it. "What did you say?"

"My friend Betsy Cummings called today." Mom dished out the ice cream. "She and Bob are just back from England and a strange thing happened while they were in London."

Oh no, I thought. Here it comes.

"They met a girl who, Betsy said, could be your twin. In fact, she was positive it *was* you at first. The girl was British, of course, but isn't that coincidence? Especially after I noticed those two kids on Mirabelle Island that looked so much like you and Davy.''

''That *was* us,'' Davy said cheerfully.

Mom smiled at him with affection. ''Davy, you have such a wonderful imagination. I think you'll grow up to write great books or plays.''

''I can write my name, and *cat,* and *bat,* and *hat,* and . . .''

That was it. The subject of Mrs. Cummings was dropped. Davy went on reeling off his spelling list while I—silently—let out a humungous sigh of relief.

I raced up to my room the moment I'd finished helping Dad do the dishes, and dressed in about a thousand layers of shirts and sweaters under my pink ski jacket. It was freezing out, so no one would think it weird that I was almost as round and padded as Frosty the Snowman. I dropped my backpack and the sleeping bag out the window, went downstairs, and said a casual ''bye'' to everyone, then collected the stuff from the bushes under my window and headed over to Carly's house.

She was ready for me. She'd borrowed (well, swiped) clothes from her older brothers for Stephen and Pat. I was taking my own sweatpants and a heavy sweater for Margaret. We stuffed the clothes, a blanket, food, and flashlight in the pack, tied the sleeping bag on, and I hoisted it onto my back.

''Okay,'' Carly said, ''I guess you're ready, but darn, I wish I could go with you.''

''So do I.'' In minutes I would be outside the castle in

Ireland. At night. Alone. "It wouldn't be nearly so scary if you came with me."

"Are you afraid?" she asked.

I nodded.

"You don't *have* to go—"

"Yes, I do." I thought of Stephen waiting in the mountains. "He's counting on me. He knows I'll come back. I'll find him and we'll be okay."

"Are you sure?" Carly's blue eyes were worried.

"Yes, I am. Now help me into the closet. It's going to be a tight fit with this pack on my back."

Pushing her clothes and junk out of the way, we squeezed me into the closet. I hunkered down with Carly's red pajamas dangling an inch from my nose, and took out the photo.

"Wait!" Carly said. "When do I call you back?"

"I don't have to be home until ten. Give me as much time as you can."

"Jenny, will you be okay?" she asked.

"Sure!" I pasted on a bright smile.

She wasn't fooled, but all she said was, "Have a good trip and tell Stephen hi from me." She swung the closet door almost closed, leaving a thin slit of light.

I studied the picture and played with my ring, thinking myself back to that high, rugged country, back to the fields of sheep and cows, back to the castle. . . .

The cold hit me first. Winter in Connecticut was nothing compared to winter in Ireland. The wind blew straight off the ocean, spitting icy bits of sleet. Clouds raced across the full moon, thick and heavy.

Up ahead, the mountains were hidden in black fog. Behind me the ancient castle reared up, totally dark and silent.

"Stephen!" I called, hoping he'd returned to wait for me. No answer. "Margaret! Pat! Stephen!"

The only sign of humans was the abandoned rental car. Sheep and cows huddled in groups, sheltering behind the stone ruins of the castle.

"Stephen!" Still no answer.

I set off across the fields, walking as fast as I could with the heavy pack. At least the exercise would warm me up.

A few minutes later I came to the stone wall Stephen had pointed to. Using Carly's super-flashlight, it didn't take long to find the note he'd promised to leave for me. It was weighted down with a heavy rock, the loose edges snapping in the wind.

It read:

I won't go too far, but I must look for Margaret. Walk a straight path, keeping the tree you see just ahead of you lined up with the tallest point of the castle, that jagged spur that juts out from the central tower.

I looked back. The moon appeared from behind a cloud and I spotted the point he meant. The tree was maybe half a football field in front of me, a single twisted pine whipped by the wind.

*   *   *

I'll be watching for you. Keep going up the mountain, call my name and I'll find you. Thanks for coming back, Jenny.

"You're welcome," I whispered.

Moving as quickly as I could, I reached the tree and passed it. A few yards beyond, I turned around and walked to the left until the top of the tree lined up in front of the jagged top of the castle. Now I had my course. I set off, checking behind me frequently to keep the two points together.

The ground began to rise sharply—I was starting up the mountain. It wasn't easy to "walk straight ahead." Rough boulders, low scrubby bushes and unexpected shallow streams kept getting in the way. I zigged and zagged, right and left, always going uphill, always checking to be sure I'd come back to the correct course.

I did okay until I reached the fog. It was like walking into a total black nothing. The moon vanished. The tree and the castle vanished.

I stopped dead, swinging the flashlight around, but the beam only went a few feet before it was swallowed up in the darkness.

"Stephen!" I yelled. "Stephen, where are you?"

My voice seemed to dissolve into the thick dark mist.

I took a few steps uphill, moving only as far as the flashlight beam lit the way, stopping, then taking a few more steps.

BOOM! A huge rolling blast of thunder shook me. A few moments later the fog lit up with an eerie glow for a split second. Lightning.

"Stephen! Stephen!"

Rain began to fall. Or maybe the fog was so thick it simply couldn't hold any more water in the air. Soft drops pattered around me.

Should I stay where I was? Should I go back? Should I go forward?

BOOM. The thunder rolled all around me. Flash! Lightning.

"Stephen! Stephen! Stephen!"

"Eeeeeee . . ." A faint howl wailed, coming from nowhere and everywhere. Where was it? Above me? Down below? To the side?

Were there wolves in Ireland?

"Stephen! Stephen! Stephen!" I stood still and cried for help. "Stephen! Stephen! Stephen!"

BOOM!!! Louder. Closer. White light blazed and died.

"Stephen! Stephen! Stephen!" I had to go down, I had to get out of the blackness. But where was he? How could I leave him to face this alone?

The howl came again, deeper, clearer. "Eeeeeeeee."

"Steeeephen! Steeeephen! Steeeephen!" My own voice was a wailing howl.

Flash! Crack! Something smashed against something. Where? It echoed all around me, coming from all directions.

"Stephen! Stephen! Stephen!"

BOOM!! Crack! Flash!

"Steeephen! Steeephen! Steeeephen!"

"Neeeeeeee! Neeeeeeee!"

A shape, darker than the darkness, loomed above me.

"Steeephen! Steeeeephen! Steeeeeee-phen!" I howled.

The shape came at me. "Jen-neeeeeee!"

"Stephen!"

"Jenny! I found you!" He was in my flashlight beam, all of him. Good, solid, wonderful, real Stephen.

His arms were around me.

BOOM!!! Flash! BOOM!!!

I wrapped myself around him, clasping my hands tightly behind his back. "Take me down! Take me down where it's safe!" I pictured solid stone walls. "We've got to get back to the castle!"

BOOM!!! Flash! Crackle! Flash! BOOM!

The world went white.

Then silent.

We lay on the ground. Stars were overhead.

I blinked, shook my head. All was quiet. The air was calm and clear. Stephen was still.

"Stephen, are you okay?" I grabbed his arm.

"I'm fine." He stirred and sat up. Then froze.

I could see him perfectly in the moonlight. He was staring down the mountain. At the castle.

The castle—the complete, whole, unbroken castle— glowed with lights. Lights shone from the towers. Lights flickered in the courtyard, moving in jerky, firefly steps. Lights spilled on stone walls that rose unbroken in the chilly night air.

A horse whinnied. A shout rang out. Someone laughed, a distant tinkling sound.

Stephen turned to me. "Do you see . . . ?"
"Yes. I see. But it's not possible . . . the castle . . ."
"Yes, the castle . . ."
We sat silently, staring at the impossible.

chapter six

"It can't be real," I whispered. "We're dreaming, or in shock. Or something."

"Yes . . . we must be . . . something," he said softly.

The bright full moon shone down on the castle below us, turning the smooth stone walls ghostly gray. The central square tower rose straight up from the moat, now filled with water. The tower was four stories tall, flanked by the two round towers, equally tall. Lights spilled from every narrow window. The courtyard was surrounded by a number of low buildings, with many more spread out beyond the walls.

At this distance I could almost pretend it was a toy castle, except that flickering torches moved back and forth and far-off voices rang out in the cold night air. A horse whinnied again and a dog barked somewhere.

"It's whole, Stephen. The walls aren't broken. This is how it must have looked in the old days." I couldn't believe what I was seeing.

He stood up. We were on a rocky ledge, halfway up the mountain. "Look around you," he said quietly.

I turned my head to the right, hoping the castle would evaporate when I wasn't looking. Trees covered the mountain that had been almost bare a minute ago. How did they get there?

"Stephen, tell me I *can't* be thinking what I'm thinking." I shivered.

"I don't want to think it either." He sounded grim. "It simply isn't possible. We can't go back in time. How could it happen?"

"Oh no," I whispered.

"What is it?"

"My ri—I mean, the magic . . . I—I might have made . . . sort of a mistake. . . ."

"What do you mean?" He frowned down at me.

"I—I was so scared. . . . I wanted to get out of there, down to the castle . . . where it was safe. . . ."

"What did you do?" he demanded.

"Nothing! I don't think . . . Well, I might have been . . . touching . . . something. . . ." I pictured myself with my hands locked behind Stephen's back, clutching the ring tightly . . . and wishing. . . . "Then the lightning hit so close to us. . . . Oh gosh, Stephen, I think I really goofed."

"Goofed!" he exploded. "That's the understatement of the century!" He stared down at the castle. ". . . Or centuries."

"Oh wow," I whispered. "*When* do you think this is? I mean, how long ago . . . ?"

"I have no idea." He reached down and helped me to

my feet. "But it seems there's only one way to find out."

"You don't mean . . . We're not going down there . . . are we?" The castle, now full of life, and all that it meant, was a little bit bearable up here, at a distance. But up close . . . I shivered again.

"Unless we plan to sit on this mountain for the rest of our lives, what other choice do we have?"

He was right. I knew it. But I didn't like it.

"Coming?" He held out his hand.

"I—I guess so. . . ."

"Let me take the pack from you," Stephen said.

I had forgotten I was wearing the backpack until he mentioned it. Now I realized the straps were digging into my shoulders and I was glad to hand it over to him.

"What did you bring?" he asked, slipping it on.

"Granola bars, a change of clothes for . . . I didn't ask you—Margaret! And Pat! Did you find any sign of them?"

He shook his head. "When the fog grew denser I turned back down the mountain so I wouldn't miss you. I might have anyway, if it hadn't been for the beam of your flashlight. I'm glad you have such a powerful one. That was a wise choice."

"Carly loaned it to me." Thinking of her made me feel suddenly, desperately homesick. Would I ever see her again? Or my parents? Little Davy . . . ?

Maybe Stephen noticed the tears that filled my eyes. He took my hand and squeezed it, then said gently, "It will be all right. We'll manage somehow."

I held his hand tightly. "Yes. We will."

"Come along, we'd better get started."

Slowly, slowly, we started down the mountain. I didn't turn the flashlight on because I felt safer covered by the darkness among the trees.

The moonlight showed us only a few stone walls crossing the fields where the sheep and cows grazed. The river was much narrower now. Here and there small huts had sprung up.

We had just reached the bottom of the mountain when we heard a shout.

"Stad!" A man came out of the night, swinging a huge ax.

I stopped, my heart racing in double time. As the man came closer I grabbed Stephen's arm and clung to it.

The man was tall and beefy. He wore a heavy cloak over a quilted tunic and leather pants. His ax glittered in the moonlight, wickedly sharp.

He growled out a question or a command in a strange language. When we didn't answer, he came closer and I got a whiff of him. Yuck! He smelled awful.

I couldn't understand a word he was saying, but his meaning was clear: who were we and what were we doing out here? Then he reached out and tried to grab the flashlight.

"No!" I said. "No, it's mine! Let go!"

He jumped back when he heard my voice. His eyes narrowed as he looked me up and down.

"Is le mise an cailín seo," Stephen said.

I glanced at him. "What did you say?"

"I *hope* I said in Gaelic that you belong to me. I don't care for the way he's eyeing you."

"Gaelic. Is that what he's speaking?" I asked, clutching the flashlight to my chest with one hand and still holding tight to Stephen's arm with the other.

"It must be. It's the Irish language, although it sounds quite different from what I learned in school. I'm sure the accent has changed over the years, but if I listen carefully I might catch a word now and then."

The man barked out an order and motioned with his ax. I didn't need Gaelic to understand we were his prisoners and he was taking us to the castle.

He hurried us through the fields. The closer we came to the castle, the more incredible it grew. The stone walls were massive, the power they radiated scary. This was no Disney imitation, although I wished with every atom in me that we'd somehow stumbled onto a movie set.

Flickering torches projected from either side of the main entrance, reflected by the water in the moat. A guard leaned on his spear, next to one of the chains attached to the draw-bridge. Over his head I could see a heavy gate suspended from the archway above, the bottom lined with iron spikes.

The guard said something to the man with the ax. His answer made them both laugh.

"Very funny," Stephen muttered.

"Did you understand them?" I asked.

"No, but I can guess what they said. And I'm quite sure it wasn't flattering."

The guard shouted and several men came running. After gaping at us with open mouths for a moment, they marched us inside the castle. I shuddered as I passed under the iron spikes in the gate above our heads. The entranceway smelled dank and moldy, as if it never saw the sun.

We came out into the courtyard, then entered a door at the base of one of the round towers. A spiral staircase wound up inside the tower. The steps were narrow and slick with moisture; there was no handrail to grab if you slipped.

Noise echoed off the stone walls, coming from above, the sound of men's voices, with an occasional bang or thud or yip-yip of a dog, and shouts of laughter. It got louder as we climbed, and the stench in the air grew stronger. The men guarding us smelled as bad as the man who had found us, but the odor flowing down the stairs was worse.

We reached the top, went down a short hall, and stopped at the entrance to a large square room. The smell was overpowering: sweat, dirt, wet dogs, rotting food and much, much worse.

The room was full of people, all men. They slouched on benches and leaned on long tables covered with the remains of dinner. One man was sound asleep, snoring, his head in a platter of greasy meat. Another tossed bones to a couple of dogs, laughing as they fought over them. Men talked, they argued, and some of them sang a faintly familiar song.

Gradually the noise died down as, one by one, they noticed Stephen and me standing in the doorway. Finally the room fell silent, except for a couple of hounds who snarled at each other.

I got a good look at the place while they stared at us. The room was two stories tall, with a narrow balcony running along one side. The walls were bare stone, except where a tapestry hung at the far end, behind several men on a raised platform. The floor was covered with rushes several inches thick. A peat fire burned in a cleared space in the center of the room, built right on top of the stone floor. There was no chimney—the smoke simply rose in the air.

"Ce híad na daoine seo?" said one of the men on the raised platform. He was powerfully built, with ruddy cheeks, a bushy red beard, and fierce blue eyes. He wore tight pants, and a white shirt with full sleeves under a brown leather tunic. I guessed he was the lord, or king, or whatever. Definitely the boss.

One of our guards answered his question, then gave us a push. It seemed we were supposed to approach Red Beard. As Stephen and I made our way past the tables, I wondered if I should kneel to him. Curtsy?

A greasy hand reached out to touch my pink ski jacket. Without thinking, I slapped the hand away. I wasn't brave—I just couldn't stand the thought of being touched. Red Beard roared with laughter, then barked out a command. No one tried to touch us after that.

When we reached the platform, a teenage boy came over to stand next to Red Beard. He looked a lot like the older man, except his hair was blond and he didn't have a beard. His eyes too were bright blue and very sharp. I figured he was the son, probably the heir to the castle.

"Cé hé tusa?" Red Beard asked.

"Taistili sinne," Stephen answered. He glanced at me and translated. "I told him we are travelers. I think that's what he was asking."

"Cad as a tháinig sibh?" Red Beard demanded.

Stephen shook his head. "I'm not sure what he's saying.

His accent is very thick compared to the Gaelic I learned.''

Red Beard barked out a string of questions—or comments—but Stephen couldn't understand him. I guessed he was asking about our strange clothes, among other things. My pink jacket, Stephen's green parka, our jeans and sneakers (mine with pink stripes) did tend to stand out in that roomful of rough, dark clothes.

Red Beard was frustrated at our stupidity in not understanding him. Then the son said something and the father gave Stephen a sharp, piercing look. From his next comment, I could tell he didn't like what he saw.

''What's the matter?'' I asked.

Sweat had broken out on Stephen's forehead. ''I caught the word *Sasanach*. It's what they call the English. The despised invaders. This could be real trouble.''

Red Beard held a discussion with his pals, but it seemed nothing was decided. Then the king noticed the flashlight I was still carrying. With gestures, he told me to hand it over.

''Should I?'' I asked Stephen.

''I don't think you have a choice.''

I gave it to him. The lord, or king, studied it, turning it over and over. It was pointing at his face when he happened to slide the switch that turned it on.

The beam shone directly into his eyes. With a roar of surprise, he dropped the flashlight. It bounced off the table onto the floor, the light sweeping the shadowy ceiling, then the roomful of men as it fell. It came to rest pointing at a corner behind the platform, lighting up a gigantic spider-web.

Instant panic. Grown men pushed and shoved as they rushed for the door. Some of them ran across the food-covered tables, sending platters flying. Dogs burst into hysterical barking, dashing around and tripping up the men.

Only Red Beard and his son stood still. The lord was rigid with rage. His son gaped at the flashlight, fascinated.

Red Beard roared out an order. His men froze in place, as if they were playing a game of statues. Another short roar and even the dogs shut up. Sudden silence filled the room.

"Cailleach!" Red Beard pointed a shaking finger at me. *"Banshee!"* He barked out a command.

Stephen and I were suddenly surrounded by men, hustled over to a doorway, and rushed down steep steps. The stairs ended in black space. We were pushed forward into the darkness and I turned around in time to see an iron-studded door swing shut behind us.

Slam! Thud! Heavy bolts slid home.

We were locked in a dungeon.

chapter seven

"Stephen, where are you?" I screamed.

"Here, right here."

I felt his arms go around me and I clung to him in pure terror. With my face pressed against his chest, I could feel his heart racing. My own heart thumped so loud it boomed in my ears.

"Tell me this isn't true," I begged. "Tell me it's only a nightmare and I'll wake up in a minute."

"It *is* a nightmare," he said. "But I'm afraid it's not the sort you wake up from."

"Oh Stephen, what have I done to us? How could I have been so stupid?"

"You didn't know.... You didn't mean to...." He went on talking in his quiet voice and I could feel some of his calm seeping into me.

After a while I loosened my grip on him slightly. "It's so dark. I can't see a thing. Can you?"

"No." He shifted his weight and I realized he was still wearing the heavy backpack. I could feel it, of course, as I gripped him around the waist, but somehow the fact of it hadn't found room in my brain to sink in.

"Food." I gave a shaky laugh. "At least we have food with us. Granola bars are better than nothing."

"Yes, except I don't feel quite up to eating, do you?"

"Not really." This place stank ten times worse than the room upstairs and that was pretty awful. "But why don't you take off the pack? At least we can sit on it." It felt like we were standing on straw, but what might be in the straw was not anything I wanted to think about.

"I'd be happy to take it off," he said. "But it will require a little cooperation from you."

"What do you mean? Oh!" I realized I was still holding him so tightly he couldn't move.

I let go and helped him ease the pack off. We lowered it to the ground and sat down on it, close together. Without being able to see, our only comfort came from touching each other. His arm was around my shoulders and mine was back around his waist. Until now the only males I'd ever touched were my father and my brother, but I couldn't imagine surviving this horrible dungeon any other way.

"Carly!" I said, suddenly remembering. "How long have I been back in Ireland? She's going to call me home before ten. What time is it?"

The dial of my watch glowed in the dark. But the hands had stopped working at 8:06. "The lightning must have damaged it. It's frozen at the time we were hit."

Stephen checked his, but it too was broken. "I'd guess

it's past nine o'clock, possibly later.''

"Good, then we only have to stand this stinking place for a little while. Unless . . .''

"Unless what?'' he asked.

The thought turned me numb with fear. "Unless she *can't* call me home. Maybe she can't reach me . . . back in time.''

"Oh, Well . . .'' He sounded as bleak as I felt. "But then, perhaps she *can.* We don't know one way or the other, so why don't we assume the best?''

"Yes . . . I guess that's a good idea. . . .'' But we both sank into a deep hole of depression.

In the silence I heard noises I'd been trying not to notice. Little rustlings, a scritch-scritch sound, then a patter-patter. Small animals? I hoped they were *very* small.

Think, Jen, I told myself, think of something to talk about. Anything to take your mind off the noises.

Finally I said, "Could you understand what the king— or lord, or whoever he is—said? He pointed to me and called me names. It sounded like caw-something, and *banshee.*''

"*Cailleach* is a woman with evil magical powers,'' he said. "Usually it refers to an old woman, but I think the king was so angry he was willing to ignore your age.''

I made myself laugh a little. "I *do* have magical powers, so I guess I can't be too insulted. Although I never thought of a flashlight as evil. Did he also say *banshee*? Did he mean like in the fairy tales?''

"Yes, the old woman who always wails just before

someone in the family dies. No one likes to see her come around, naturally.''

''*Now* I'm insulted. He can't really think I'm a *banshee,* can he?''

''I guess he—''

Thunk! Bam! Bolts or locks were sliding. The door opened.

The sudden brightness hurt my eyes. Stephen and I stood up, moving as one person.

A guard held a torch for an old lady. She was so tiny the top of her head only came to my chin. A heavy hooded cloak covered all but her wrinkled face.

She gazed into my eyes for a moment, then looked down at my ring. With gestures, she told me to hold out my hand.

''*No!*'' I blurted out. Pure panic swept over me. We couldn't lose our only hope of getting home. ''Not my ring! You can have anything but my ring!''

The guard growled something, then pulled a knife from his belt. The long blade flashed in the torchlight.

''Go ahead, stab me!'' I shouted, too scared to think straight. ''I am not giving her my ring!''

The old woman spoke for the first time. Her voice was gentle, musical. She apparently told the guard to put his knife away, then she took a step toward me. Her eyes looked right into mine and I immediately knew she wasn't going to hurt me.

I slowly held out my hand. She didn't touch the ring. Instead, her hands, twisted with arthritis, hovered over it, moving in a circular pattern. After a moment she gazed into my eyes again, said something, then turned and started up the spiral stairs.

The guard barked out an order.

"He said 'Go,' Jenny," Stephen shouted with joy. "We're supposed to follow her."

I glanced at the guard. He motioned me toward the stairs. Stephen grabbed up the backpack and we almost ran out of that terrible place.

We climbed up and up, until we reached the top floor of the castle. The lady led us into a large square room, apparently the living quarters. A dozen women and children stopped talking and stared at us and our strange clothes.

There was very little furniture: a canopy bed, a couple of chairs and a few stools, some chests, a table, and a spinning wheel.

Rushes covered this floor too, with another fire built on bare stone in the center of the room. A little smoke escaped through a small hole in the roof, but a lot stayed in the room, turning the air bluish.

The women, children, and even the three small dogs, watched us with curiosity, all idly scratching themselves. While the old lady took off her cloak, she spoke to a young woman, maybe twenty-something, who held a baby. She was tall, with greasy blond hair pulled back into a bun. Both women wore heavy long gowns of brownish-black wool and gold pendants engraved with unusual designs.

None of these people were especially clean, but if I lived in a smoke-filled room, I might not be either.

The young woman handed the baby to a young girl and came toward us. She smiled at me, then gestured toward the ring. I held it out without hesitating this time. Like the old lady, she didn't touch it but held her hands over it for a moment.

"*Bandraoí rionaí isea tu,*" she said. It sounded like "bandree ree-o-nee isha two."

I glanced at Stephen, hoping he understood.

"Queen," he said. "She called you queenly, and also a woman of magic, a witch. But it's not meant in a bad way. It seems to be a title of great respect."

"How do they know?" I asked. "How did they guess about my ring?"

"I'm not sure," he said. "Perhaps they have an instinct for magic. Perhaps they have some powers of their own."

"Maybe they do. . . ." I said slowly, remembering how the old lady had instantly made me understand she wasn't going to hurt me.

The young woman smiled. "*Is mise Marra.*" She pointed to herself and said again, "Marra."

"Marra," I said. "Is that her name?"

"Yes," Stephen said.

She smiled and nodded, encouraging me.

"Marra." I pointed to her, then at myself. "I'm Jenny. Jen-ny. And this is Stephen. Ste-phen."

She repeated our names, then curtsied to me! I was so surprised I didn't know what to say. I was still in shock when she led me to one of the chairs by the fire. It was totally weird to be suddenly treated like such an honored guest.

The old lady sat in the other chair. She nodded at me, almost a bow, but more as if she was accepting me as a person of equal status. Placing her hand on her chest, she said, "Alainn."

I bowed back to her and repeated, "Alainn."

One by one, the others in the room were presented to me, like I was actually a queen. Stephen stood beside me, and by catching a word of Gaelic now and then, and with many gestures, we figured out a little about the family.

Alainn was the mother of the king, or *rí,* as they called him. She was only about fifty years old, although she looked twice that, and a *bandraoí*—a wise woman, or a witch woman.

Marra was married to the *rí,* and was the mother of the baby, Thady. And she was only sixteen! She was the *rí's* third wife, the stepmother of four children. The oldest, Finnin, was the blond teenager we'd seen earlier in the hall. He was seventeen, a year older than his stepmother!

The other children belonged to the *rí's* sister, Rosin, and the other women were servants.

I noticed that the more Stephen talked, the easier the Gaelic became for him. He was tuning into the accent and remembering more words.

Then Alainn asked me the question I'd been dreading: where did we come from?

"Stephen, we can't tell her the truth," I said. "How can we say we come from the future?"

"They already know you have special powers," he said. "I'll try to explain that we came through magic."

"Don't mention my ring. I can't admit it to anyone, even if they've already guessed. Actually, Alainn didn't guess— she *knew* immediately. She looked in my eyes, then went straight to my ring. How did she do that?''

''She's Irish. She believes in magic. No, that's not quite correct. To her, and all the Celtic Irish, it isn't a matter of believing or not. Magic simply *is*. It exists just as trees exist, or cows, or the ocean.''

''I think I see what you mean,'' I said. ''I wouldn't say that I *believed* in trees, because they're a fact. They're real.''

''That's right.'' Slowly, with many gestures, he tried to answer Alainn's question. I heard him at one point say, ''America,'' and ''Vineland,'' pointing to the west and making a wavelike motion with his hand, then he said, ''Brendan.''

Alainn nodded and he told me, ''I think she understands. An Irish saint named Brendan is said to have sailed to America—what the Vikings called Vineland—in the 500s, almost a thousand years before Columbus. The New World was known to the Irish long before southern Europeans began exploring it.''

Marra pointed to our sneakers and clothes, especially my jeans. She'd probably never seen a girl in pants. Stephen thought a moment, then stood up and mimicked mounting a horse and riding off.

''I've never been on a horse in my life!'' I said. ''You shouldn't have said that. What if they expect me to ride?''

He grinned. ''Then hold on tight and try not to fall off.''

''Thanks a lot!'' I gave him a playful punch.

Everyone laughed when they saw us fooling around and one of the little boys raced around the room on a pretend horse. Now several of the women and girls found the courage to touch our clothes, indicating ''soft'' and ''pretty.''

They all scratched themselves from time to time and I figured their heavy wool clothes must be awfully itchy.

We had unzipped our jackets, but kept them on. In spite of the fire, the big room was cold. The tall, narrow windows were covered with what looked like an oily thick paper, but the wind worked its way in anyway. Drafts swirled the smoke around, and also the unpleasant odors that seemed to fill the castle. Once in a while an extra strong gust from one direction would bring a whiff of something worse.

I began to understand part of the source of the problem when one of the smallest children, who toddled around bare-bottomed in spite of the cold, felt nature calling. His mother, Rosin, whisked him out of the room, but not before some of the damage was done. A servant calmly went to a basket of rushes and, taking up a good handful, spread them over the spot. How many layers of what were buried in the rushes?

Alainn said something and everyone fell silent. She turned to me and asked a question. She was quite serious and I knew what she was saying was important.

"*Ríon*. Queen." Stephen translated as he caught certain words. "Powerful—most powerful . . . evil witch . . . fight . . . English . . . Tudor woman . . ."

Alainn demonstrated drinking something, then clutched her stomach and fell limp. Coming back to life, she repeated, "*Eilís.*" It sounded like "I-leash." She made stirring motions with her hands, then pointed to me and said, "*Bandraoí rionaí.*"

"Jenny!" Stephen was excited. "I think she's asking if your magic can fight the evil queen Elizabeth! She must mean Queen Elizabeth the First! That tells us approximately where we are in time. Elizabeth's army invaded Ireland in the late 1500s. That must be now!''

"The 1500s?" I said. "That's more than four hundred years ago. Are you sure?"

"How can I be sure?" he said impatiently. "But that's what it sounds like."

Alainn was waiting for an answer. They were all waiting, looking anxious and scared.

"What can I tell her?" I asked. "I don't want to disappoint them, but what can I say?" I frowned, thinking hard. "Tell them . . . tell them I'll try. Say I'm not sure because Elizabeth is very powerful, but I'll do my best."

"That's a good answer," he said. "Her troops nearly destroyed this country during the invasion. They're right to be afraid of her, but perhaps it would help ease their worries if they had a bit of hope."

"That's about all I can give them—hope," I said. "Tell them I'll try."

When Stephen got the message across, smiles broke out. Gosh, it was scary to be in a position where my promise meant so much to these people.

Several of the children began to play pretend soldiers and the women began to chatter. Marra gave an order and one of the servants brought in loaves of bread and a thick cabbage soup. Stephen and I were starved by then, and while the food wasn't great, it filled our stomachs.

Our little party was interrupted by a gruff voice. The *rí*, Donogh McSheehy, stood in the doorway. Beside him was Finnin, his blond son. Finnin held Carly's flashlight and Donogh McSheehy was boiling mad.

chapter eight

The red-bearded king stomped into the room. I jumped up from the chair. He looked me up and down, gave Stephen a glance of contempt, then shot a sharp question to his mother, Alainn.

She answered him gently, and the conversation that followed was clear to me, without knowing a word of Gaelic. He thought we were dangerous creatures who belonged in a dungeon. She disagreed. He told Finnin to show her the magical light that burned without heat. Finnin turned the flashlight on and gave it to her.

The women gasped and stepped back, but they relaxed when Alainn calmly took the flashlight. She examined it with curiosity and decided it confirmed her belief that I was an extremely talented witch.

Marra stood to the side, holding baby Thady, while this went on. When Alainn explained to the king just how wonderful my powers were and what a terrific witch-queen I was, Marra nodded, siding with her mother-in-law.

McSheehy's annoyance began to fade. He gave me another long look. I could practically read his mind. It had finally occurred to him that it might be a smart idea for the *rí* to keep such a fantastically wonderful magical person as myself in his castle.

But I sure wasn't ready for this powerful, intense, red-bearded king to go down on one knee and bow his head to me!

"Gosh, Stephen, what do I do now?" I said with a touch of panic.

"Say *'Go raibh maith agat.'* " Stephen grinned. "It means thank you."

"Go raibh maith agat," I said.

The *rí* stood up and gave Finnin an order.

Finnin's answer sounded exactly like, "Gee, Dad, do I have to?"

The answer was yes.

Finnin, pouting, dropped to his knee and made what might have been the shortest bow in history. But when he stood up, he winked at me. What the heck did that mean?

Then Donogh McSheehy scowled at Stephen. He said something to Alainn, spitting out the word *Sasanach.*

Stephen went pale. "Jenny, whatever happens, don't ever admit that I'm E-n-g-l-i-s-h. We are their enemy and they despise us. Maybe he suspects me from the way I pronounce the Gaelic words, or perhaps it's the way I look. Whatever it is, if he finds out the truth, I'm dead."

I turned to the *rí.* "Stephen no *Sasanach.* No, no." I shook my head firmly. "American, like me." Pointing west, I made the wave motion with my hand. "Over the ocean. America. Vineland. Americans *like* the Irish." I blew a kiss in his direction.

McSheehy frowned, puzzled.

Finnin snickered. Elbowing his father, he said something, gesturing at the room.

Stephen turned stiff with anger.

"Take it easy," I warned. "What did he say?"

"Piteanta," he muttered. "He's implying that because I'm up here with all the women and children, he doubts my . . . er, well . . . He thinks I'm a sissy."

I started to giggle but quickly turned it into a cough. Stephen was in no mood to appreciate the humor.

The *rí* barked out an order, pointing to the stairs.

"Now what?" I asked Stephen.

"He wants me to sleep downstairs in the main hall with the rest of the men. I think it's so he can keep an eye on me, in case I'm an English spy."

"But you can't!" I grabbed his arm. "We have to stay together, in case Carly calls us home. Maybe she can't find us four hundred years in the past, but if she *can,* we have to be touching or I'll go back alone. Stephen, we can't be separated for even a minute!"

"How can we argue with the king's order?"

I thought for a moment. "If he believes I'm a powerful witch-queen, maybe he'll listen to me. Tell him . . . tell him . . . I need you near me because . . . your mother is also an important witch and . . . I'm supposed to guard you with my magic. If anything bad happens to you, your mother will attack the castle with her evil spells."

Stephen, knowing that the *rí* was watching him, tried not to laugh. "That's slightly ridiculous."

"Well, can you come up with something better?" I felt a little huffy.

"Maybe my mother-the-witch needs you to stay near me to . . . increase your powers?"

"That's it!" I said. "She's added her magic to mine, through you. And, of course, I want to use all my possible powers to protect the king and his castle."

"It's a little far out, as they say," Stephen said. "Why don't we just tell him we're married instead?"

"Oh, yeah, right." I punched his arm. "The last thing I need right now is a husband!"

"Are you turning down my proposal?" he said, grinning.

"Stephen, get real! We have a serious problem here!"

He glanced at the *rí,* who was still scowling at us. "You're right. Okay, Plan B it is. Here goes."

He faced the king, but also explained the situation to Alainn. I watched her reaction, since I was pretty sure her son would listen to her advice when it came to magic.

To my incredible relief, she nodded several times. I guess the idea of combining magical powers made sense to her. Maybe it was something she'd done herself.

McSheehy's eyes were narrow with suspicion as he listened. I suppose you don't hang on to a castle and a kingdom too long if you're the type who's easily fooled by strangers. But when Alainn added her opinion, he finally grunted out his permission for us to stay together.

Stephen and I tried not to show how pleased we were.

Marra's baby had begun to fuss. She'd been patting his back, but now she handed him to his father, the *rí*. Baby Thady gurgled and grabbed at the bushy red beard. Tough old McSheehy suddenly melted like snowflakes in the sun. He tossed the baby up, then covered him with kisses. Little Thady cooed with delight and the king cooed back.

Everyone in the room began to relax.

Marra gave me a grin that said, "Don't worry, I know how to manage *him*."

Finnin stalked out of the room in disgust.

Alainn opened a chest and took a stringed musical instrument out of a soft leather bag. It was about two feet tall, made of glossy carved wood. When she tuned it, the notes flowed out, mellow and pure.

Everyone smiled and settled down to listen, including the *rí*, who sat by the fire with the baby on his lap. Alainn began to sing as she plucked the strings and the room filled with music.

"It's the Irish harp," Stephen whispered to me. "Remember the McSheehy legend, Jenny? She learned from the *file* after she saved his life."

I nodded. The McSheehy legend had said that listening to Alainn was like hearing the angels sing. It was true. The rich, delicate tones of the harp rose and fell with her clear voice, each note seeming to float in the air before drifting along to blend in with the others.

She was clearly telling a story they all knew and loved. Even the children nodded along with the music, occasionally breaking into smiles of delight or sad frowns of sorrow. The harp's rich wood gleamed in the firelight as Alainn's long fingers drew the melody from it as if by magic.

We were actually hearing the harp Pat had told us about. It seemed incredible. It *was* incredible.

Alainn sang for a long time, then struck a final chord and said something that apparently meant, "It's time to go to sleep." She slid the harp back into its bag.

With sighs of protest, the women rose and began to bustle around, sliding a trundle bed out from under the canopy bed and unrolling sleeping pallets that had been stored in a corner.

Stephen and I looked at each other, wondering what came next. Alainn took charge. As we tried to tell her how much we enjoyed her music, she led us to a staircase opposite the one we'd come up. Down a few steps, a room opened off a landing. It was just large enough for a canopied bed and a chest. Two servants had followed us, one carrying our backpack, the other the flashlight, which she presented to me with a deep curtsy.

"You know, Stephen," I said, "I kind of like being a queen, even if it's a witch-queen. To live in a castle and listen to music like that . . . Plus, I've never been curtsied to before. I could get used to it."

"You might have to," he muttered.

"Don't say that!" The good feeling the music had given me vanished in an instant. "Why are you suddenly so crabby?"

"The *rí* spoke to me when you weren't looking. One wrong move and I could be in a lot of trouble."

"Then watch your step," I snapped at him.

He only shrugged.

Oh wow, what was wrong with me? "I'm sorry, Stephen. Really. I just want to keep on feeling good for a while."

"I know, this whole business has us both on edge. It's my fault. My moods keep going up and down like a hot-air balloon. I'm sorry too. Why shouldn't you enjoy being Queen Jennifer while you can?" He patted my hand. "Fair Queen Jennifer, I bow to your beauty and grace."

"Thank you, kind sir." I smiled.

A few minutes later I almost changed my mind about the advantages of being a queen. One of the servants showed me to what we Americans normally call a bathroom. There was *no* resemblance between the two. Let's just say that the "facilities" consisted of a narrow bench over a deep hole in the thick stone wall. And that was it. I won't even mention the smell. You can imagine.

Back in "our" room, I was glad to see that someone had brought a jug of water and a bowl for washing, although there was no soap. Stephen left to take his turn with the nonplumbing.

I shoved the sleeping bag against the headboard to use as padding to lean on. The pillows were rock-solid and the mattress full of bumps and sags. I lifted a corner of the covers and checked. The mattress was only a large bag of coarse cloth stuffed with straw. No wonder it felt so lumpy.

Stephen came back and closed the door, looking grumpy again. He was right. His moods were shooting up and down like a roller coaster.

I tried to cheer him up. "It's okay, Carly might be calling us anytime now. It has to be almost ten o'clock in Connecticut."

"I'm sure it's long past ten." He sat on the foot of the bed. The servant had left one candle on the chest. It threw flickering shadows on his face, making his worried frown seem ominous. "I think we have to give up hoping she'll be able to reach us."

"Don't say that!" I put my hands over my ears. "We *can't* be stuck here."

"I thought you liked being a queen."

"Well, it's not all peaches and cream." I scratched an itch on my elbow, thinking about the "bathroom." "Besides, I'm sure we'll get home somehow. I know Carly. She won't give up, even if she has to call me all night long."

"But if she can't reach back in time—"

"Stephen, please stop thinking the worst. What's the matter with you?"

"I'm worried that McSheehy suspects my background. It wasn't only Elizabeth the First who sacked this country, but many other British rulers too. The Puritan Cromwell was perhaps the worst. He literally leveled Ireland, burning or blowing up every single castle, fort, house, and hut he came across. Thousands of people were slaughtered."

"That's horrible."

"Yes, it was, so please be extremely careful not to use the word *English*—or *British*—around these people." He scratched his leg.

"I promise." I rubbed my itchy arm. "But I still think we might be zapped back home any minute, so maybe we won't have to worry much longer. Why don't you move closer so you're touching me, just in case."

He shook his head, smiling a little. "You won't give up, will you? I admire you for it, Jenny." He scooted up a little so his leg touched my foot. "Pardon me, *Queen* Jennifer."

I grinned. "That's more like it." Now my other arm itched. I began to realize that I'd been feeling itchy for quite a while but had been too busy to pay much attention.

"Then there's Margaret." Stephen frowned again. "So much has happened to us, but I haven't forgotten that she and Pat are still lost in the mountains. And we're no help to them whatsoever."

"Maybe someone else has found them. Or maybe they weren't really lost, or they've managed to get down by themselves anyway."

He gave me a half grin. "Stop trying to make me feel better. I can see what you're up to and it won't work."

"Are you sure?" I smiled back, scratching my stomach.

"What the . . . ?" Stephen stood up suddenly and stomped his leg, then he began to scratch like mad. "It's crawling on me."

The moment he said it, I felt several somethings crawling on my skin. Whipping off my ski jacket, I pushed up the sleeve of my sweater. Red bumps dotted my arm. I tried to swat a tiny black bug, but it jumped away.

"Fleas!" Stephen said. "We're covered with fleas!"

"Oh gross! *Super-gross!*" I felt them on my legs, my back, in my hair. "Eeuw! Get them off me!"

"How?" He tried to catch one on my arm, but fleas are fast. "It's all the dogs. The rushes must be loaded with fleas." He made another grab. "Missed it!"

I pictured Carly handing me a white box. "The first-aid kit! Maybe it has insect repellent." I snatched up the backpack and emptied it on the bed. Grabbing the box, I popped the lid open. "Yes, here it is. Does this stuff work on fleas?"

"I hope so." He was already peeling off his sweater.

I squirted some gunk in my hands, then gave the bottle to Stephen. He tore off his shirt and rubbed the repellent on his chest.

I coated my arms, face, and neck, even rubbing the stuff in my hair. Who cared what I looked like? This was an emergency.

"Close your eyes, Jenny," Stephen said. "I have to take off my trousers."

"So do I. We've got to cover ourselves all over with this stuff. Why don't we blow out the candle?"

"We have no way of relighting it." He turned his back and undid his belt buckle.

"Stephen, wait!" That was as far as I wanted him to go. "I'll hold up the blanket I brought, then you do the same for me." I grabbed it off the bed and shook it out.

"Good idea, but no peeking."

"Are you kidding?" The blanket was too thick to see through, but I still turned my head to the side while he undressed. That was when I spotted another tube in the first-aid kit. "We're saved! There's anti-itch cream too."

"Fantastic." He grabbed it. "I'm not much of a gentleman. I should have let you go first."

"Yes, you should have. Hurry up so I can have my turn." The heck with being polite. I was going insane with those fleas crawling all over me.

A few minutes later we were both slathered with spray and cream, dressed in the clean clothes I'd brought for Margaret and Pat. We sat on the bed, trying not to scratch the spots that itched in spite of the cream. It was a losing battle. Fleabites are fierce.

I glanced at my watch, then shook it. It was still stuck at 8:06, when the lightning had zapped us into the past. "How late do you think it is?" I asked him.

"Well past midnight. At least it feels that way. I'm dead tired."

"So am I. Poor Carly. What's she thinking now? And my parents! They'll be so mad that I'm not home. They're probably giving Carly a hard time about it. What's she going to tell them?"

"I don't know, but she's a wonderful fibber. She'll think of something." He scratched his chest, then yawned. "I'll be in trouble too when my father finds out I'm gone, but right now I don't want to think about it. I'm going to try to sleep."

He reached for the sleeping bag, but I stopped him. "If you lie down on the floor, you'll be turning yourself into a flea feast, repellent or not. Besides, we really should be touching—just in case."

He grinned. "You're an extremely persistent person, Jennifer Delaney." He spread out the sleeping bag. "Crawl in here and zip yourself up. I'll wrap up in the blanket you brought."

That's how we spent the night. Itching, scratching, dozing, waking, itching, scratching, dozing . . . Waiting for Carly to call us home. Waiting for the sun to come up.

chapter nine

Carly didn't call us home, but the sun at long last came up.

I was tired, itchy, and grouchy. So was Stephen. We grumbled at each other while we took turns coating ourselves with more repellent and cream. Then we rolled up the sleeping bag, crammed our stuff into the backpack, and went looking for breakfast.

The table had been moved near the fire. To my surprise, it was covered with a linen tablecloth, and they all used linen napkins to wipe their grimy hands.

"They don't wash their hands," I whispered to Stephen, "but they have linen my mother would die for. That's weird."

Before he could answer, they greeted us and offered us food.

No one had individual plates. Instead, cheese and meat were served on wooden platters. They broke off pieces with unwashed hands and helped themselves to flat, round oat-meal cakes, dipping their fingers into a bowl of butter to spread on the cakes.

I whispered to Stephen, "Haven't they ever heard of germs?"

"As a matter of fact, no," he whispered back. "Germs weren't even suspected to exist until the late 1800s. We really can't blame them. They have no idea of the connection between dirt and disease."

"Well, if we stay here much longer, I'm going to teach them a little basic biology." I surprised myself by sounding exactly like my mother.

Stephen and I each took one of the flat oatcakes but skipped the butter. I bit into mine. It was dry and hard and gritty. A servant brought us metal mugs of something cloudy and bitter to drink. Stephen guessed it was a type of ale. I sipped a little and nibbled a little to be polite, planning to pig out on granola bars later.

I watched Marra, wife of the king, fussy baby in one hand and breakfast in the other, sitting in this smoky, smelly, cold, stone-walled room. Being a queen in real life was definitely *not* peaches and cream, no matter what the fairy tales say.

Shouts sounded from the staircase and McSheehy jumped up from the table. Several soldiers stopped in the doorway, supporting an exhausted teenager. He was spattered with mud and his dark eyes were full of fear. He gasped out his message, then collapsed. Two soldiers carried him away.

The king barked out orders, then rushed down the stairs with the rest of the men.

The women went into action, breakfast forgotten. The fear on the messenger's face had spread to everyone in the room. Several of the children began to cry, but no one had time to comfort them. They were too busy packing up bags and baskets.

"What's happening?" Stephen asked Marra.

"Tá an Sasanach ag druideam linn." She continued taking linens out of a chest.

"Did you understand that?" I asked Stephen.

"It's the English army." He knelt by a little girl with tears running down her cheeks and patted her on the back. "They're getting closer to the castle."

"Why are they packing up? Isn't the castle the safest place to be?" I scooped up a toddler who was dashing around, bewildered by the excitement, getting in everyone's way.

"Perhaps they're preparing to leave if the castle is taken. But I'm sure they'll try to defend it."

The *rí*'s sister, Rosin, shouted at a little boy who was tugging at her skirt. He wailed, and Rosin only shouted louder.

"Come on, Stephen," I said. "Let's be useful."

We rounded up the children and took them down to the far end of the room near one of the tall, arched windows. The paper-covered opening was set into a recess, with a large U-shaped window seat in front of it. I settled the children on the cushions and Stephen brought a platter of food over. We helped them finish their breakfast and the business of eating dried up their tears.

"Do you know any Irish songs?" I asked Stephen. "Once they've finished, they'll be restless again."

" 'Danny Boy'?"

"That's too sad. How about 'When Irish Eyes Are Smiling'?"

Stephen and I were singing loudly, watched by the puzzled but pleased children, when Finnin appeared. He said something to Alainn and she gave an order to the servants, who all left at once.

Finnin strolled over to us, smirking. He was delighted to catch Stephen playing baby-sitter. Whatever he said contained the word *bean*—woman. Stephen refused to translate. His face turned red with rage.

"That decides it." He watched Finnin leave. "I'm going downstairs to help the men."

"Stephen, you have to stay near me. If Carly calls us back—"

"Carly *can't* call us back. If she could, she would have already. We're stuck here, Jenny. You might as well face it."

I put my hands on my hips. "I won't give up! I won't!"

"Then don't." We glared at each other, then he smiled slightly and touched my cheek for an instant. "Please try to understand, Jenny. If I have to live here, I can't spend my time with only women and children." He walked away.

Alainn suddenly gave a loud cry. At first I thought she was reacting to our quarrel, but then I realized she hadn't even noticed us. She dashed out of the room and down the stairs.

Stephen followed her, so I hurried after him. If he wouldn't stay near me, *I'd* have to keep close to *him*.

The next floor down, we spotted Alainn in a small office off the great hall with her son the king. They were having an argument. It seemed like a good day for fights—everyone was doing it.

Stephen had stopped to listen and I caught up with him. Alainn wanted McSheehy to do something and he didn't want to do it. She kept pointing to the mountains we could see outside the narrow window. The opaque stuff that covered the windows upstairs had been torn off here and the cold wind blew in. I guessed that the king wanted to keep a watch for the approaching English soldiers.

Alainn's gentle voice grew more demanding. Then she opened a small chest and lifted out two cloth bags. From the way she handled them, I could tell they were heavy.

Stephen glanced at me and I nodded. We both remembered Pat's story about the buried treasure.

Alainn opened the high neck of her dress. She pulled out a thick gold chain from under her clothes and took it off. Untying one of the bags, she opened it. We caught a glimpse of pearls, rubies, and more gold. Adding her chain to the collection, she retied the bag.

McSheehy pointed to the gold pendant she wore outside her dress. She shook her head, then gestured toward the mountains again. McSheehy shook *his* head, refusing to do as she wanted. She turned around in frustration and saw Stephen and me standing in the doorway.

I began to apologize for eavesdropping, but she grabbed my hand and pulled me into the room. She gestured at me, then herself, then me again. I caught the words *bandaoí rionaí* repeated several times.

"What's she saying, Stephen?" I asked.

"She says her magic will protect the jewels, but with your added powers, the treasure will be completely safe up in the mountains. I think she's also trying to convince him it's only for a short while, until he fights off the English army."

"Oh gosh, we know how that turns out, don't we?" I felt suddenly terribly sad, knowing that this powerful, strong king was going to die soon. I thought of him playing with his baby son and had to swallow a hard lump in my throat.

Should we warn him? Beg him not to fight the English? But why would he believe us? And should we even dare try to change the course of history? I decided to talk to Stephen about it when I had a chance.

The argument over the jewels went on for a while, but Alainn won, as we knew she would. In spite of her gentle manner, she was a very determined lady.

A manservant took us down to the busy courtyard. The entire castle was bursting with activity. Soldiers were riding out to carry the message to the countryside. Men and dogs were rounding up sheep and cattle from distant fields, and women, including the family servants, were out harvesting the winter vegetables, mainly cabbage, potatoes, and onions.

The noise was incredible. Soldiers sharpened axes and knives on a shrieking grindstone, blacksmiths hammered horseshoes at a forge, sheep and cattle bawled as they were herded into pens, and everyone shouted to be heard in the confusion.

The manservant had left us in the entranceway, telling us to wait. He returned, leading two horses. Another man followed with a third horse. They were sturdy animals, with broad backs, strong legs, and big hooves.

"Oh no," I said. "I don't know how to ride. I can't get on one of those things."

"I'm sure you can *get* on," Stephen said. "The question is, can you *stay* on?"

"Very funny." I studied the beasts, trying to decide which was the tamest. "Quick, tell me. What's the secret to riding, Stephen?"

"I have no idea. I've never been on a horse either."

"Oh, great." I didn't have time to worry about it. One of the men led me to a mounting block, brought a reddish-brown horse over, and the next thing I knew I was sitting in the saddle.

That was one wide horse. My legs could barely straddle him. The servant adjusted the heavy stirrups and stuck my feet in them. The saddle was hard, but at least it was padded with a sheepskin.

The servant led my horse away from the block, then let go of the bridle! Now what? My horse was free to do whatever he wanted!

It turned out all I had to do was sit there because the horse stood still.

"Good horsey," I said. "Good boy." I patted his neck.

The horse started walking. "Help!" I shouted. "What do I do now?"

"Use the reins," Stephen said. "You've seen it in the movies. Pretend you're a cowboy."

"That's easy for you to say, standing on the nice safe ground." But I pulled back on the reins and the horse stopped.

Hey, this was kind of fun. I touched his sides lightly with my heels and the horse started walking again. This time I tried to steer him. When I pulled the reins to one side, he turned! I was riding a horse!

"Good show, Jenny," Stephen said.

We turned right, my horse and I, then left, then we went around in a circle. "Nice boy," I crooned. "Good boy."

Stephen laughed. "Jenny, if you'll take a closer look, I think you'll find she's a mare."

"How can I tell from up here?" I shot back. But I changed my tune to "Good girl."

Stephen mounted his, a black with a white blaze down his nose. We both practiced riding around the busy, noisy courtyard while we waited for the others.

Finally Alainn appeared, carrying her Irish harp in its leather bag and a heavy red wool blanket. She slung the strap of the harp bag around her neck and tied the blanket onto her saddle.

Stephen and I nodded at each other. We were about to witness where the oldest harp in Ireland was going to be hidden in the mountains.

chapter ten

Donogh McSheehy appeared with another man who looked a lot like him, red beard and all. I'd seen him enter the castle with his family while I was riding around, and guessed he was related to the *rí*.

The king glanced at Stephen mounted on his horse and began to shout. One of the servants led Stephen back to the mounting block and I realized McSheehy had ordered him to get off.

"No, no," I said, trying to sound firm. It's not easy to contradict a king's orders. "Stephen has to come with me."

The *rí* growled something, motioning Stephen to get down.

"If he doesn't go, I don't go." I steered my horse over to the other side of the block and began to get off.

Alainn shook her head at me. I stopped, half on, half off the saddle. It was a very uncomfortable position.

She spoke to the king, clearly insisting I come along.

Bandraoí rionaí was repeated several times.

McSheehy pointed to Stephen and used the hated word *Sasanach*.

I slid back into the saddle to wait while they argued it out. I remembered Pat saying that part of the McSheehy family believed two strangers had gone along when they buried the treasure. Two. That meant me *and* Stephen. Alainn would win this battle also. Donogh McSheehy may have been a king, but I guess even kings have to listen to their mothers sometimes. Especially when she's a lady as determined as Alainn.

Finally the *rí* shouted out an order and a servant hurried away. Then McSheehy turned to the man who looked like him and began what sounded like a long list of instructions. That fit Pat's story too. The king had temporarily given command of the castle defense to his brother and gone to the mountains when the treasure was hidden. Now I knew why: I wouldn't go without Stephen, Alainn needed my help, and the *rí* was coming along to keep an eye on the suspicious stranger who might be an English spy.

An old man with white hair rode up to us, leading a huge gray horse. This man had to be McSheehy's most trusted servant, according to what Pat said. It was weird to see a story you'd been told come to life right before your eyes.

McSheehy didn't bother with the mounting block but swung himself up into the saddle. At last we were off.

One by one, we followed the king through the entrance-way, over the drawbridge, and out into the fields. Rain clouds were moving away, and the damp countryside sparkled in the sun.

I was last in line. Thanks to Stephen's explanation of my jeans, they assumed that I knew how to ride.

My mare and I were doing fine until McSheehy's gray horse broke into a trot. Instantly, all the other horses followed his lead.

"Whoa!" Bouncing up and down, I grabbed the saddle with one hand and pulled back on the reins with the other. My good-girl horse ignored me and kept up her trot.

Bounce-bounce-bounce. My head jerked up and down. Thud-thud-thud. My bottom collided with the saddle. Jiggle-jiggle-jiggle. My insides shook like jelly.

Stay on the horse, Jen, I told myself, just stay on the darn horse. It's a long way to the ground. I dropped the useless reins onto the horse's neck and clung to the saddle with both hands.

Field after field, on and on we trotted. After a while I found that if I braced my feet in the stirrups and pushed myself up when the horse went up, and let myself down when the horse went down, it wasn't so bad. But it took a lot of concentration. There was no time to look at the scenery.

Whoops! I was almost thrown onto the horse's neck when she suddenly slowed to a walk. We had reached the bottom of the mountain.

I relaxed a little as we started up a sloping path. Compared to a trot, a walk was definitely a nicer pace.

Up ahead of me, Stephen twisted around in the saddle and called back, "How are you doing, Jenny?"

"Great!" I said. "No problem. How are *you* doing?"

"I won't be able to sit down for a week!"

I laughed. "You win. You're a lot more honest than I am. I'm sore all over, plus I'm starving." My stomach growled, as if agreeing with me.

"Me too. I wish we'd brought some granola bars, but I suppose we'll have to wait."

I saw Alainn up ahead and realized she was riding with both legs on the same side of the horse. I'd read about that. Ladies in their long skirts had to ride sidesaddle. How the heck did she stay on while we were trotting? At least I was wearing pants, so they'd given me a regular saddle.

We climbed up and up, and kept climbing. Finally the horses stopped beside a small waterfall. I was glad to get off Good-Girl for a few minutes. While the horses drank from the deep pool, Stephen and I strolled over to an opening in the trees.

From here we could see great sweeps of the country spread out below us. It was awesome. The air was so clear we could see forever. The river ran past the castle and all the buildings and huts clustered around it, then dropped down into the valley, where it flowed into several lakes before finally running into the sea.

Above us, the sky was huge. Great white clouds sailed along, blown by the cold wind that never seemed to die down. The sun shone in the crystal air, but out at sea a few dark clouds were moving in, probably bringing more rain.

"We should be checking for landmarks, Stephen," I said. "Then, when we get back to our own time, we'll be able to locate the treasure, once we know where it's hidden."

"I suppose so." He didn't sound enthusiastic.

"Come on, cheer up," I said. "We'll get home somehow, I know we will."

He said nothing, only stared out at the land below us, absentmindedly scratching a fleabite.

"Will you help me note the landmarks anyway? Just in case? Pretty please with cheese on top?"

He laughed a little. "What on earth does that mean?"

"It's something my mother says. At least it made you smile."

He turned to me and took my hands. "Jenny, you are amazing. If I have to be stuck somewhere in the sixteenth century, I'm glad I'm with you."

"Yeah, but if it weren't for me, you wouldn't *be* stuck here." Heck, why did I have to remind him?

"True enough." He grinned. "But I'm still glad it's you."

Alainn called me. With gestures, she asked me to come with her. Stephen and I followed her up to the top of the waterfall. We found a natural spring, where the water bubbled up from the ground.

She asked me a question.

"What did she say?" I asked Stephen.

"I think she said this is a sacred place and she wonders if you believe there's enough magic here to protect the jewels and the harp."

Alainn pointed to a fairly shallow cave.

"She doesn't realize that the treasure will be here for at least four centuries," I said. "Not just a few days. We'll have to help her find a place that has much more protection."

"Why don't you perform some sort of ritual before you tell her no?" Stephen suggested. "It would be much more impressive."

"Like what?"

He grinned. "I don't know. You're the witch-queen."

"It's your idea," I said, but decided he had a point. After a moment I held out my hands, moving them over the spring in flat, shallow circles, as if sensing the degree of magic offered.

Alainn watched carefully.

Inspired, I made up a little rhyme. "Magic, magic, what's your pleasure? Is this the place to hide the treasure?"

I moved over to the cave and repeated the same ritual, chanting the rhyme with a little more confidence. I "felt" for the magic a moment longer, then shook my head at Alainn. "I'm sorry. We'll have to look for a better place."

She nodded and we returned to the horses. McSheehy was waiting impatiently, and was not pleased to be told we were moving on. I couldn't blame him. With the English coming, he belonged back at his castle, but I knew we had to find a hiding place that would survive for centuries.

Our next stop was beside an ancient twisted tree. Under the knarled roots was a hollow deep enough for the jewels and harp, but the tree wouldn't last many more years.

This time, as I performed my ritual, a strange thing happened. For a moment I felt a soft tingling in my hands. Alainn had said the tree contained powerful spirits. Was it possible I was actually sensing them? Of course not, I told myself, but I decided to repeat the ritual anyway, to see what happened.

This time I asked the question very seriously. "Magic, magic, what's your pleasure? Is this the place to hide the treasure?"

My hands tingled a moment, then the feeling passed. "Weird," I whispered to myself.

I shook my head, and we rode farther up the mountain. A rocky crag jutted out over a deep ravine at our next stop. I was afraid that once the trees were gone, leaving the mountain bare as it was in our time, the stones, solid as they seemed now, might be washed away by erosion.

Again I performed the ritual. Again my hands tingled softly, then the feeling faded.

McSheehy muttered dire threats as we remounted the horses, so I was glad when we stopped at the perfect spot. In a thick growth of pine trees, a deep cave led into the side of the mountain. It was low, only about three feet high, but the rock walls seemed solid and the entrance was almost hidden by a large boulder.

I went through the ritual again. My hands tingled for a full minute after I asked the magic question.

Shaken, all I could do was nod. Yes, this was the right place.

Alainn was watching me. I met her eyes and saw that she knew. She smiled with understanding.

McSheehy handed the two bags of jewels to his white-haired servant. The old man crawled into the cave and disappeared. When he came out, he indicated that the treasure was well hidden deep inside the mountain.

Alainn took the harp out of its bag and cradled it in her arms for a moment. It gleamed in the sunlight. Holding it gently, she began to play and sing.

It was a sad, sad song. She was saying good-bye to her most precious possession, her gift from the famous poet. Her lovely voice rose and fell in the mountain air, spinning a spell over all of us. Even a sparrow in a tree cocked his head and listened.

The song came to an end. Alainn returned the harp to the bag and wrapped it in the thick red blanket, then crawled into the cave with it. I was glad she didn't know yet that she would never see it again.

It was a long ride back to the castle. I tried to memorize any landmarks I thought might survive the next centuries— rock formations, the angle of a valley, the shape of the mountains around us. It was difficult to see because of the thick trees, but I was determined to do what I could to help Pat, another musician, find the harp way off in the future.

If we ever made it home to tell him.

Partway down the mountain the trees thinned out a bit and we saw the view below us. A steady stream of people the size of ants crawled toward the castle. They drove pigs, goats, sheep, and cattle. Horses pulled carts piled high with possessions. Everyone was rushing to the safety of those thick stone walls.

At the bottom of the mountain, instead of trotting across the fields, McSheehy kicked his horse into a canter. The next thing I knew, Good-Girl was rolling along behind him, with a terrified me clinging to her back. This was a heck of lot faster than a trot. I grabbed the saddle and closed my eyes so I wouldn't see the ground flying past.

At last we slowed down. The peasants made way as we clattered across the drawbridge and into the courtyard, now crowded with people and their things. When I dismounted, I staggered a bit. My leg muscles felt like they'd turned into wet spaghetti.

Donogh McSheehy leaped off his horse and, shouting orders, ran into the castle. Stephen and I followed at our own pace, both of us walking with sort of a rolling gait, like the old-time cowboys in the movies.

We climbed up the spiral staircase. As we passed the great hall the king's voice rang out. He was already into a fierce argument with a number of men.

When we made it up to the family quarters, we found confusion there too. The room was filled with women and children. Alainn had arrived before us and she was greeting everyone with hugs and kisses. I figured they must be assorted relatives looking for safety in the castle.

Everyone talked at once and the children raced around playing games, shrieking with laughter. The English army seemed almost forgotten during what had turned into a family reunion.

Marra sat in one of the window seats, her baby on her lap, her face pale, her eyes huge. Stephen and I went over to her.

"Cad é an nuacht?" he asked.

Marra answered but Stephen frowned, not understanding. She repeated certain words slowly, using gestures.

"It seems that an important lord, the Earl of Desmond, has asked McSheehy for help with the English," Stephen said. "He thinks he has them trapped and needs reinforcements."

"But if McSheehy is gone, who will defend the castle if the English break out of the trap?" I asked.

"I think that's why Marra is frightened." He asked her another question and she answered. "The king's brothers want to ignore the message, but she thinks her husband will decide to join Desmond. She's afraid he'll be killed."

As soon as he said the words, we looked at each other. We *knew* he'd be killed.

"We have to try to stop him, Stephen," I said. "We have to warn him."

"I doubt he'll listen to us."

"We have to *try*."

He turned away, thinking. "What if he *does* listen to us? Then we'd be meddling with history. If he lives, the story as we know it, our history, would be wrong. That means our time, the future, would be different. If we change history, what will happen to the future?"

He had a good point, but how could we ignore a man's life? "We can't say nothing, when we know what's going to happen to him."

We stared at each other, knowing we were both right. What should we do?

I tried to remember Pat's story exactly as he told it. "Wait a minute! All Pat said was that the king was killed by the English after he buried the treasure. He didn't say *when* exactly. It could be weeks, or months from now."

"That's true," Stephen said slowly. "Perhaps this isn't the time. It might not hurt to warn him."

"Let's go." I started for the staircase, with Stephen right behind me.

The noise and confusion in the great hall was ten times worse than any school lunchroom. Men shouted and banged on the tables, dogs barked with excitement. McSheehy sat on the raised platform, arguing with what had to be his brothers. The four of them looked so much alike, they could have been quadruplets.

Stephen led the way, pushing past the tables. He stopped in front of the *rí* and waited until he noticed us. It only took a minute.

McSheehy glanced at us, then glared at us, thunder in his eyes. It was obvious he thought we had a lot of nerve. Who were we, a couple of strangers? How dare we interrupt an important, if loud, conference?

He roared for silence and the room went still. Talk about being in the spotlight! I could feel all those eyes boring into my back.

Stephen spoke slowly, one word at a time. *"Tugaimíd comhairle duit. Ta fios ag an bandraoí. Má théann tú ar an cath seo beidh tú marbh."*

McSheehy stared, then began to scream at us.

We stood there, stunned.

"What did you say to him?" I asked Stephen.

"I think—I hope—I said that the witch-queen knows he will die if he fights the English."

"What's wrong with that?" I wondered.

McSheehy, still furious, continued shouting at us.

Stephen shook his head, not understanding.

The king took a deep breath, settled down, and repeated

very slowly, *"Is fear mé. Níl eagla orm roimh bás. Ní rithe mé o'n Sasanach ar nós caoira."*

Stephen translated. "He's a man and he's not afraid to die. He won't run from the English like a sheep."

A cheer went up from the men, except for two of Donogh's three brothers.

Stephen said, "I think we've just accomplished what we tried to prevent. His mind is made up. He's going to fight with the Earl of Desmond."

McSheehy barked an order. A couple of guards grabbed us and began to hustle us out of the room. Not the dungeon again, I thought. Please not that!

At the doorway the *rí* barked another order. The guards stopped.

The king spoke slowly again. Stephen turned pale.

"What did he say?" I asked, terrified.

"W-we—you and I—are going into battle with him."

chapter eleven

"We're going into battle?" I squeaked. "Us? But we're just kids!"

"And you're a girl," Stephen said. "He can't do this." He called to McSheehy across the room, *"Cé'n saghas rí a chuireann cailíní go coga."* He whispered to me, "I asked him what *rí* sends girls to war?"

The king's answer contained the now dreaded words *witch-queen.* I wasn't surprised when Stephen told me I was supposed to use my magic against the English army, and, of course, at the same time protect McSheehy and his men.

"I don't have that kind of power," I said. Then I remembered the way my hands had tingled on the mountain. I'd never suspected I'd had *that* power either.

"Don't worry, Jenny," Stephen said. "We'll manage . . . somehow."

The guards let go of us, but ordered us up the stairs to

the living quarters. I figured we were supposed to get ready to leave whenever McSheehy said it was time to march.

In the short time we'd been gone, food had appeared on the table and everyone was clustered around it. I was absolutely starving, but I couldn't go near the food touched by so many unwashed hands. Stephen and I went into "our" room and we each ate several granola bars. What would we do when they ran out?

We were both jumpy, expecting the message to come any minute: it's time to go to war. It was frustrating. All we could do was wait—and worry.

As soon as lunch was over, Alainn seated herself by the fire and, with Marra's help, began to treat the visitors for a variety of problems. As she worked Alainn spoke to Marra, teaching her the art of *draiocht leigheas*, healing witchcraft.

Jittery and scared, I kept glancing at the stairs, expecting a soldier to come and drag us away on the king's orders. I was glad nothing happened, but in a way it would have been easier to get it over with.

With nothing else to do, I watched Allain, and after a while I began to get interested.

Selecting from baskets of herbs and roots, she used different combinations for rashes, infections, headaches, and stomachaches. Some herbs were brewed into teas, others wrapped in scraps of cloth that were then soaked in various bowls of liquids and applied like a bandage.

But before she prescribed for each patient, she first looked deep into their eyes, then, not quite touching them, moved her hands over the entire body, just as she did my ring. Sometimes she knew what was wrong immediately, other times she repeated the process, "feeling" carefully.

"What do you think, Jenny?" Stephen asked me. "Is it only an act she's putting on?" Apparently he'd begun to find it fascinating too.

I remembered the tingling in my hands up in the mountains. "No, it may sound crazy but . . . it's not an act, I'm sure of it." Maybe someday I'd tell him about what I'd felt at the sacred spots, but not for a while yet.

"Maybe Alainn can help us," he said. "The king listens to her. She could tell him he shouldn't send a witch-queen to war."

"Good idea," I said.

The moment Alainn finished treating everyone's aches and pains, we took her over to one of the window seats, where it was fairly quiet. Stephen told her that McSheehy wanted us to go along when he went to fight with the Earl of Desmond.

To our surprise, Alainn thought it was a good idea.

"She says I can now prove to Finnin that I'm a man, if I'm brave in battle," Stephen told me. "She even said I'm fortunate to have the chance!"

"Yeah, lucky you."

"Don't forget, Jenny, Alainn is terribly nice, but she's a part of these times. We can't expect her to think the way we do. She can only be what she is, an Irish lady of the sixteenth century."

"I know, you're right."

Stephen put his arm around my shoulder. "And she said it's good you're going with her son and his men. She thinks you'll be able to protect them.''

"But I can't. I can't stop a war. No one can, and in a war people get hurt and killed.''

"Wouldn't it be wonderful if you could stop all wars?'' he said, hugging me.

"Yes,'' I said quietly. "I'd love to have that kind of magic.''

I looked at the stairs again, but still no one came to get us. The afternoon was dragging on. I hated the idea of leaving, but the wait was almost worse. I had to do something to keep my mind off it.

I looked around the crowded, smelly room and it suddenly hit me that, in a way, I had a type of "magic" that might be helpful to these people. Just as Alainn knew which plants cured which problems, Stephen and I knew how to prevent some of them. I told him my idea.

"Well, you can try,'' Stephen said. "I'm not sure they'll listen, but it can't hurt.''

We asked Alainn to join us again, and also Marra. They sat in the window seat, little Thady asleep on Marra's lap, and listened as Stephen did his best to translate.

"In my country, America,'' I said, "we have a special magic to fight evil spirits.'' I pointed to a fleabite on the baby's arm, then pretended my stomach and head hurt. They nodded, understanding.

"Evil spirits can live in the rushes, in clothes, in straw beds, in dirt. We fight the evil spirits by washing them away. We throw out the old rushes often. We take them outside and burn them. Then we scrub the walls and floors with hot water before we bring in clean ones.''

Marra said something. "She wants to know where you find so many rushes," Stephen said.

"Um, well . . ." I thought a moment. "Tell her we grow lots and lots—acres of them—also straw and hay."

Marra nodded and I went on. "We also take our clothes to the river—often—and wash them with soap. Do they have soap here?"

Stephen asked and they said yes, but not much.

"We make lots and lots of soap, and we scrub the clothes hard." I mimicked scrubbing and rinsing. "And we wash the bed sacks too, then put in clean straw. Now all the evil spirits are gone from the house—I mean, castle."

Alainn and Marra were listening carefully.

"There is one more thing," I added. "Evil spirits, called 'germs,' live on our hands, and we don't like to put germs in our mouths. So we wash our hands—with soap—before we eat."

They looked shocked and Alainn asked a question.

Stephen said, "She wants to know if you mean *every time* before you eat."

I nodded. "Every time."

They began to talk to each other, speaking so quickly Stephen couldn't follow them. "I think you may have asked too much, Jenny. It's a radical idea for them."

I shrugged. "Well, at least I tried."

Alainn and Marra stopped chattering, thanked me with polite smiles, then moved away, still discussing these weird magic rituals.

A few minutes later a soldier came up to announce that the *rí* and his troops were finally ready to leave.

Stephen and I looked at each other. ''Don't worry,'' he said. ''We'll be all right.''

I nodded, feeling almost numb. The time had come.

The women and children poured down the stairs to say good-bye to their husbands, fathers, and brothers and sons.

While Stephen went to get our backpack, I glanced around the room, and suddenly realized I'd forgotten to tell Alainn that if they'd build a chimney over the fire, the room wouldn't be so smoky. Well, maybe I'd survive the war and be back. I'd learn Gaelic and—

''Ready, Jenny?'' Stephen said, returning with the backpack.

''I guess so.'' My stomach turned over with a sudden jolt of fear.

The courtyard was chaos. Peasants milled around as soldiers on horseback called out orders. Carts loaded with supplies rumbled over the drawbridge. Some women cried while others tried to hold back tears as they said good-bye to their men.

Marra looked up at her husband, Donogh McSheehy, on his huge gray horse, her face sad. He reached down, took the baby from her, and kissed him good-bye. Handing him back, he spoke briefly to Marra, and said ''*Slán,*'' but didn't kiss her. She turned away and went inside.

What would happen to her? I wondered. When the *rí* was killed, she'd be a sixteen-year-old widow with a baby. Maybe she'd marry again, or go home to her family, if she had one. I wouldn't have traded places with her for anything in the world.

Finnin was riding a beautiful white horse. He caught my

eye and winked, then pulled out a sharp dagger and pretended to stab imaginary enemies as he demonstrated to me how he was going to kill the English. I saw Stephen watching him and thought how much more grown-up, how much more of a man Stephen already was, compared to this kid who was showing off.

One of the soldiers handed Stephen a sword, but the *rí* noticed and shouted an order. The soldier took it back. The king wasn't going to let the *Sasanach* have a weapon, even if he was dragging him into battle.

Finally McSheehy, with Finnin and two of his brothers at his side, moved out at the head of the soldiers. A man brought over horses for Stephen and me.

"Not again!" I groaned. "I've barely recovered from our ride this morning."

"Would you like me to ring up a taxi for you instead?" Stephen asked.

"Yes! Please!"

I took a good look at this horse while he tied the backpack behind my saddle. She was a dark brown mare, but not nearly as large as Good-Girl. Stephen's horse was small too, and kind of bony. It looked like we'd been given the leftovers, with the best horses going to the soldiers.

Alainn came up to me when I was mounted. I tried to say good-bye and thank you. She smiled, then touched my ring, covering it with her veined hand. For a moment my finger throbbed with heat. Alainn was adding some of her magic to mine. It was true, then. The power could be shared.

The white-haired man who had gone to the mountains

with us appeared, riding the same horse he'd had before. Alainn spoke to him, then us.

Stephen translated. "His name is Angus, and he'll look after us. Alainn told him to take good care of the witch-queen, but I suspect his main job is to keep an eye on me, the suspicious foreigner."

"Good thing too," I said. "You're up to no good, anyone can see that."

He raised one eyebrow. "Don't blow my cover, kid," he said, leering like a movie villain.

We said good-bye to Alainn and rode over the draw-bridge, falling in behind the foot soldiers who made up the main body of McSheehy's army. To my surprise, a few women walked with them, each with a weapon of her own, as well as cooking pots and bags loaded with supplies.

Each man carried two or three weapons—either long-barreled pistols, muskets, huge axes, swords, daggers, leather slings, pikes, or spears. They wore chain-mail shirts or padded leather vests, backpacks, and slung sacks of ammunition and food over their shoulders.

The sight of all those horrible weapons made me shudder. This was real, too real. Stephen and I were actually going to war.

Angus kept us at the end of the slow-moving line. That was fine with me. No trotting, no cantering, just a nice slow walk across the beautiful Irish countryside.

It's a good thing I didn't know how slow, and how long, that walk would be. Rain began to fall, a soft mist at first, then a downpour. I was drenched. We kept going. Sunset, then darkness, came and I waited for someone to say, "Halt. Make camp." No one said it.

My legs had turned numb, then my backside. I shivered in my wet ski jacket, then the shivers passed and I guess the rest of me had gone numb. We kept riding. The rain let up, then came down again. We kept going. The rain stopped and the moon came out. We went on.

Is it possible to sleep on a horse? Yes. I nodded and dozed, only catching myself when I was about to slip off. I'd hooked my hands around the saddle, and after a while I'd automatically pull myself back upright, not even bothering to really wake up. It was a long, long night.

A distant *pop-pop* worked itself into my dreams. It was the Fourth of July at home. We'd driven to the beach to watch the fireworks, but they were so far away we couldn't see them. Everyone wanted to get closer, except me. Dad started the car and I tried to tell him that I didn't want to go. He wouldn't listen. The booms grew louder. I kept begging Dad to turn around and take us home, but he didn't.

BANG BANG BANG. I jerked awake. The sky was light. The sun was up. The mountains had vanished and we were in rolling hills. Irish hills.

Ahead of us, the horses at the front began to canter. The foot soldiers began to jog. My mare broke into a trot. What a lousy way to wake up!

Donogh McSheehy's men let out blood-chilling screams as they followed him over the top of a hill and disappeared from sight. The foot soldiers broke into a run, spreading out across a field where sheep grazed. Bleating and baaing, the sheep scrambled to get out of the way.

Angus yelled something and swung his horse to the left.

We followed him to the top of a rocky ridge.

Down below was a wooded valley, with a shallow river flowing through it. The English in their metal helmets and vests were on the far side, firing cannons and guns at the Irish scattered through the woods. There didn't seem to be many Irishmen, but they were dressed in browns and blacks and blended into the cover. They were smart enough to use the trees as protection while they fired at the enemy.

McSheehy's men flowed down the slope, still yelling like fiends, shooting as they ran. The English shot back and began to advance across the river, dragging the cannons with them.

Stephen and I jumped off our horses and crouched behind a rough boulder. I'd seen all I ever wanted to see of war. The noise was awful. I didn't know if the screams meant anger or triumph or pain. Holding the reins, I covered my ears, but I couldn't block out the sound of booming guns and those horrible cries.

Angus, still on his horse, said something to me. He was probably saying now was the time to use my magic. I nodded and he raced off down the hill.

My hands shaking, I played with my ring, wishing and hoping the fighting would stop. No matter what I tried, the noise went on and on. My magic wasn't enough to halt a war.

The bangs and booms grew louder. It sounded like the British were driving the Irish up the ridge toward us. A bullet bit into a rock not six feet away.

I screamed, ''We've got to get out of here!''

"Right!" Stephen said. "Quick, let me help you on your horse."

Terrified, I leaped for the mare, wishing she could take me straight back to Connecticut. I hated it here! I wanted to go home!

Stephen was shoving me into the saddle when a cannon ball smashed into the rock beside us.

The entire world exploded. I fell and fell and fell into a black endless hole.

chapter twelve

I opened my eyes but saw nothing. I heard nothing. I was lying on my back and something heavy pressed down on my legs.

Then I heard a distant boom. A few seconds later white light flickered, faded, and the world went black again. Why was it so quiet? Where were the screams? The yells?

Stephen! Where was he?

"Stephen!" I shouted.

The weight on my legs shifted and groaned. "Jenny, are you all right?" he asked, pushing himself away. "That cannonball hit so close to us. . . ."

I sat up. "I'm okay. At least nothing hurts. What about you?"

"I'm fine, but where are we?" He was only a voice in the darkness. "What happened? Where did everyone go?"

"Good question." I felt around, touching grass and small stones. "We're outside, it's cold, and it's night, but I don't see stars or a moon.'' Wondering how late it was, I automatically checked my watch. ''It's working! Stephen, my watch is keeping time again. It says eight-oh-seven.''

''So does mine!''

A horse whinnied right behind me. I felt its soft nose nudge my hand. ''It must be the mare! You were helping me on her when the explosion came.'' Grabbing the bridle, I stood up and felt behind the saddle. ''Our backpack is here! That means we have a flashlight!''

I unzipped the pack, dug out the light, and turned it on. Luck was with us; the battery was still strong. The beam found Stephen just as thunder boomed in the distance. Several seconds later a flash of lightning lit up the sky. The scene was instantly familiar.

''Stephen, I think we're back! We're back in our own time!'' I threw my arms around him.

''You're right, Jenny,'' he said, hugging me. ''This is the same fog, the same thunder and lightning, as when we left.''

''No more battles! We're home!'' I thought briefly of Marra and Alainn, but it was so good to be back where we belonged, I tried to put them out of my mind.

''It's amazing, this fog . . . it's just as it was when we were thrown back into the past.''

''Oh wow, Stephen . . .'' I looked at my watch again: 8:08. ''Have we come back to the same time we left? Even though we spent two days and nights in the sixteenth century?''

''I think we must have. Perhaps that's why our watches didn't work,'' Stephen said. ''Time literally stood still while we were gone.''

"Wow, that's weird." I shivered. My clothes were still damp from the rain that fell in the 1500s.

The horse nickered and I patted her neck.

"It looks like you brought along a souvenir," he said.

"You poor thing, zapped four hundred years into the future." I continued stroking her. "I hope you like it here because there's no way I can take you back. At least you'll never ride into another battle." I shuddered, remembering.

"I wonder how the fight turned out," Stephen said.

"I don't know . . . it was so horrible, all that screaming and killing. I want to forget it." But I knew I'd always remember Alainn and Marra, the castle and the music of the harp, blond Finnin and red-bearded Donogh McSheehy. . . . "I don't think I ever want to travel in time again."

"Nor do I," he agreed.

My stomach growled. I was starving. It was hard to calculate when our last meal was, but you could say we hadn't eaten in four hundred years. I dug out the granola bars and divided them between us. We ate silently. I guess we were both still a little dazed, as well as more than a little exhausted.

I'd just started on my third bar when I heard a faint sound. "What was that?" I whispered, swinging my flashlight. The noise came again. *Eeeee-en.*

"That sounds like Margaret!" Stephen said. "I'm sure it is! How could I forget? She and Pat are still lost up here in the mountains." He cupped his hands and shouted her name, "Mar-gar-et!"

Eeeee-en. The voice came from all directions, but guessing she was above us, I directed the flashlight beam up the hill.

"Come on," Stephen said. "Let's go find her!"

The horse stepped in front of the light and I saw the ancient saddle and bridle. "Okay, but we'd better hide these first."

Stephen knew exactly what I was talking about. We'd been through so much together, our minds seemed to be tuned in to the same station. It was hard to believe I'd only met him a week ago.

He continued calling Margaret while we whipped off the saddle and bridle and stuffed them behind a bush. Someone, maybe the Irish kid, Mickey, would find them later, but we'd be back home by then. I hoped.

"What about the horse?" I said. "We can't leave her alone in the dark. She could fall and hurt herself."

"Do we have a rope?" he asked.

"No, but we could tie the extra clothes together to make one." That's what we did, working quickly. Our knotted shirtsleeves and pant legs made a weird, but workable rope that we slung around her neck.

I'd propped the flashlight on a rock so its beam would face uphill, and each time she called, Margaret's voice was a little louder. Now, staring into the darkness, I thought I saw a pinprick of light.

"Is that her?" I pointed out the light to Stephen.

"Yes, must be. Let's go!" He shrugged on the backpack and set off up the slope. I followed, leading the horse.

Margaret's light bobbed around as she made her way down to us. The black fog around us seemed less dense. Either we were moving out of it or it was drifting away.

"Stephen!" Margaret called. "Is that you?"

"Yes, of course," he shouted. "Who else would be insane enough to come looking for you?" He was joking to cover up his relief at finding her.

She appeared in the flashlight beam. She looked great with her hair flying every which way and a smudge of dirt highlighting one of her cheekbones. How did she do it?

She stopped and crossed her arms. "I knew it. He follows me everywhere. I can't get away from my baby brother even when I lose myself in the Irish mountains." Then she ran to Stephen and threw her arms around him.

He hugged her back. "Sorry to be such a pest. I'm quite relieved to see you too. Are you all right? Where's Pat?"

"I'm fine, but he's hurt his ankle. We think it's sprained. We're camped up over there." She pointed to a high ridge.

The fog was disappearing quickly now and the moon shone through, lighting up the snow-streaked mountains rising and falling around us.

"Hello, Jenny," Margaret said. "It was good of you to come along. And what's this?" She noticed the horse for the first time. "Why, how clever of you! A horse will be a terrific help in getting Pat out of these forsaken mountains. But what made you think to bring one? What's his name?"

I decided to answer her last question, and hoped she'd forget to ask the first one again. "It's a mare," I said. "And her name is . . . Bonnie Girl." I don't know where that came from, but as soon as I said it, I liked it.

"She's a sturdy little thing, isn't she?" Margaret said, patting her. "We'd better get started. Pat will be wondering."

"What happened to you?" Stephen asked as we headed for their camp.

"That awful fog came down on us," she said. "It was just like a cloud settling over our heads. We were in a valley and there were mountains all around us. We became turned around somehow and weren't sure which direction to take. Then Pat slipped and twisted his ankle. He's far too heavy for me to carry, even if we knew where we were headed. We had plenty of food and camping gear, so it only seemed sensible to stay put and wait for someone to find us."

"You made the right decision," Stephen said. "I suspected something like that might have happened. But why did you leave Pat to come looking for us?"

"We thought we heard voices calling. The fog was beginning to lift and we decided I should chance it. I didn't want our rescuers getting lost in these mountains too."

Stephen and I glanced at each other. We'd been lost all right, four hundred years in the past.

A few minutes later we crossed over the ridge and saw Pat's campfire twinkling in the dark. It wasn't long before we were warming our hands over it. The heat felt great. Patches of snow lay around the camp, but for the first time in ages I began to feel warm.

Pat was glad to see us, especially Bonnie Girl. "I'd been wondering how I'd manage to limp out of here. What made you think of bringing a horse?"

Uh-oh, that question again.

"Er, well . . ." Stephen began. "We, er, thought that one of you might be injured. . . ."

"Yes," I said. "And when we got to the castle, we met this Irish kid, Mickey, and he had this horse, so we asked to borrow it."

"But why does it have a rope of clothes around its neck?" Margaret asked, laughing.

"We, uh . . . lost the first rope," I said. "It's a long story. Don't you think it's time we started back? Pat needs to get to a doctor."

Pat groaned. "It's not going to be a pleasant trip, even on horseback." But he began to put out the campfire and Margaret started taking down the little pup tent.

"It's not terribly far, you know," Stephen said, helping her. "Just over this ridge and down the mountain. If it hadn't been for the fog and Pat's ankle, you'd have been back at the car long ago."

"But think what an adventure we'd have missed," Margaret said gaily.

Stephen and I exchanged looks again. We'd had enough "adventure" to last us a long, long time.

Margaret had made a rough splint for Pat's ankle, in case it was broken. We helped him onto Bonnie Girl and began the trip back.

The fog was entirely gone when we started down the mountainside overlooking the castle. In the bright moonlight we could see the ruins of the towers and the massive stone walls. To my relief, it was dark and silent again. Still, I felt sad, thinking of the people who had once lived there. What had happened to them, especially Marra and Alainn? Would I ever find out?

When we reached the rental car, Pat collapsed on the

backseat with a gasp of relief. He'd been trying to hold in his groans the whole way down.

"Let's go find a doctor," Margaret said. She helped toss the gear into the trunk, then slid in behind the wheel and started the car.

That's when I remembered.

"Stephen and I forgot to tell you," I said casually. "We think we know where the McSheehy family treasure is hidden."

Margaret stomped on the gas in surprise and the motor roared. "Where is it?"

Pat sat up straight. "Yes, where? How do you know?"

Oh wow, I hadn't planned ahead. How could I answer this question?

"We—we . . . uh, found a, uh, cave, when we were looking for you in the fog. At least, I did. I didn't have time to check inside, but I, uh . . ." What did I do? "I . . . shone my flashlight in and I think I saw something. But I'm not sure."

"Why didn't you take time to inspect it?" Pat asked.

"Well, uh, Stephen was calling me and I . . . well, it was kind of spooky. Anyway, I thought one of you should rescue the harp, since you're McSheehys."

"That's true." Pat leaned back, satisfied. "But the moment the sun comes up tomorrow, Jenny, you're going to take us to this cave."

Whoops! That's when I realized I had a major problem with the magic.

chapter thirteen

"Um, could you wait a minute, Margaret?" I said. "I have to talk to Stephen."

"Hop in," she said. "You can talk while we drive."

I had to think fast. "I—I can't come with you. My . . . my parents are picking me up."

"I see." She was peering into the backseat, her eyes on Pat's pain-streaked face.

"Y-yes, they gave us a ride up here to the castle and they'll be picking me up soon." Wow, what a stupid idea. What kind of parents would drop their kid off at a castle late at night to wander around the mountains?

I was lucky. She wasn't listening. Her mind was on Pat. I finished, "So I need to talk to Stephen before he leaves."

She turned off the motor. "All right, then."

I led Stephen over to the castle wall. "Remember the rules of the magic?" I said. "No matter when I leave home,

I arrive at each new place every three hours, until I jump ahead eighteen hours.''

"Yes, that's what we figured out."

"I've only come here to Ireland twice! The first time, when we came together, it was late afternoon. Then when I came back for you it was about seven-thirty in the evening."

"I get it," he said. "That means it will be ten-thirty tonight when you return."

"And that's less than an hour from now. Then the next time it jumps ahead eighteen hours, to late afternoon. This stupid magic has the craziest rules."

"What you need is a different picture, one taken in the morning, so you'll return then," he said. "But how to find one?"

"Wait a minute! Margaret may have it. The photo of the castle was missing from the album, remember?''

"Good thinking, Jenny. I'll ask her."

We went back to the car. I held my breath and crossed all my fingers, hoping she had it, and it would work.

She did and it would. Stephen and I decided by studying the angle of the shadows that it was taken about nine or ten in the morning. We made plans to meet then. I waved as the three of them drove off to find a doctor for Pat.

While I waited for Carly to call me back, I turned Bonnie Girl loose in a grassy field with a stream running through it. For a second I thought about taking her home with me, but Carly would pass out from shock if a horse suddenly appeared in her closet.

"Hurry up, Carly," I whispered. "I can't wait to get home!"

I blinked my eyes. Ireland was gone. I was back in Connecticut.

"Wow, what happened to you?" Carly asked, standing over me. "You're a mess. What have you been doing?"

Living in a smoky castle—learning how to ride a horse the hard way—climbing up and down mountains—charging into battle . . . it would take hours to tell the whole story.

I scrambled to my feet and gave her a hug. "I promise I'll tell you absolutely everything, Carly, but I can't right now." It was great to see her, but I was aching to get home. I'd been wanting to the whole time we were stuck in the sixteenth century, and now—at last—I could.

"Come on, Jen," Carly begged. "Tell me a little. I've been waiting so long."

I opened the door to the hallway and went out. "Did you watch that movie *Back to the Future, Part 99*?"

"Yes. Why?"

"I've never seen it, but I'll bet I have a better story for you." I reached her front door. "I'll tell you every single detail tomorrow. Thanks for calling me back, Carly. It's great to be here." I opened the door and ran down the sidewalk.

"What time tomorrow?" she yelled after me.

"I'll talk to you in school!" I shouted.

As tired as I was, I jogged all the way home. When I turned the corner and saw my house, it looked so familiar, so welcoming, I felt tears come to my eyes. I thought I had myself under control by the time I went inside, but just the smell hit me hard. All houses have their own special aromas, and now I savored this, my very own special, beloved, dear *Home*.

Dad was paying bills in front of the TV. An old-time movie was on the screen. Horses reared, swords clashed, guns boomed. I cringed.

Dad was so involved with his calculator, he didn't even glance up at me. "Hi, honey, how's the science project coming?"

"It—it's fine. We got a good start tonight," I said, promising myself that Carly and I would work on it for sure this weekend. "Where's Mom?"

"In the kitchen, making school lunches."

Of course, I thought, just as she does every night. It was all so *normal*. So right. "Tell her I'm taking a shower, okay?"

"Sure." He was deep into his checkbook.

When I got to the bathroom and looked in the mirror, I was glad he hadn't seen me. I was filthy. Soot and dirt were smeared on my face, my hair was limp and greasy, my clothes torn and stained. I wondered if my ski jacket would ever be pink again.

Stepping into the shower was pure luxury. It's a miracle, I thought, all this delicious hot water, sparkling tiles, shiny faucets, plus plenty of soap to wash away the dirt of centuries—literally.

I was shampooing my hair for the third time when I remembered the white lie I'd told Dad about the science project. I'm not used to lying to my parents.

But ever since I discovered that my garnet ring could take me anywhere, I'd been telling one lie after another. I had to, to keep the secret, I told myself.

And look what happened, Jen, I argued with myself. You didn't mean to, but you took Stephen into real danger. We could both be rotting away in the dungeon. We could have been thrown by a horse, or hit by a bullet. We could still be stuck in the sixteenth century. We could have stayed in the past forever.

And our parents would never know what had happened to us. Carly would have no way of knowing either. To them, we would have simply disappeared. We'd just be . . . gone.

And all the time my parents are trusting me, believing in me.

I rinsed the shampoo out of my hair and turned off the water. I was bone-tired, but the shower had helped revive me. As soon as I'd thrown on pajamas and a bathrobe, I went down to the kitchen. Mom had finished packing the lunches and was making a casserole for tomorrow night's dinner.

"Mom," I said, taking the milk jug out of the fridge, "did I ever meet my great-grandmother Ophelia?"

"Only once when you were a tiny baby, but you wouldn't remember that." She drained the cooked macaroni into a colander. "Why do you want to know?"

"I was just curious." I poured a tall glass of milk. "I love the ring she gave me, and I wondered if you could tell me about her. You know, what kind of person she was.''

"She was my grandma and I adored her,'' Mom said. "But she wasn't always easy to live with. She could be very charming, but she was also quite stern. Rules were rules and *would be obeyed.* One rule that no one ever dared violate was to enter her room when she had one of her headaches. Only her maid was allowed in. Grandma would get headaches from time to time, and she had to be left completely alone until she felt better.''

I smiled into my milk, wiggling my ring finger. I had a good idea just what caused those ''headaches.''

"But don't misunderstand,'' Mom went on. "She was a lot of fun too. She had a wonderful collection of costumes from all over the world and when I was little we'd play dress-up. She'd let me try on Indian saris, Mexican skirts, Japanese kimonos—all sorts of beautiful clothes.''

"You told me before that sometimes she'd speak in different languages,'' I said.

"Yes, she had her flighty side too.'' Mom mixed the macaroni in with leftover meat and vegetables. ''Words and phrases would pop up in the middle of a conversation and I'm not sure she even realized she was speaking Chinese or Greek, or whatever. If anyone mentioned it, she'd deny it, so we learned to simply ignore it.''

Maybe it was a good thing I hadn't had time to learn much Gaelic. "She sounds like an interesting person, but . . . well, I wanted to ask you . . . did you trust Ophelia?''

"Trust her?'' Mom laughed as she sliced up mushrooms.

"With my life. In fact, I owe her my life. When I was two years old, I fell into a pond. By the time they scooped me out, I had swallowed a good bit of water. Grandma Ophelia gave me mouth-to-mouth resuscitation until I began breathing again.''

"I thought mouth-to-mouth was a recent invention." If Mom was two then, that had to be about forty years ago.

"Maybe Grandma invented it on the spot," Mom said. "I have no idea, but I wouldn't be here if it weren't for her."

"Neither would I, I guess." I took a long drink of milk. "Mom, can I ask you something?"

"Sure." She added the mushrooms to the casserole.

"It's about . . . well, trust. Like, I always felt you and Dad thought I was a pretty okay kid, and well . . . you sort of trusted me to be good and stuff.''

"Jenny, darling, do you want to talk woman-to-woman?" Mom turned to face me. "Ask me anything you want about boys and I'll try to answer you honestly.''

"Oh! No!" I felt my cheeks flame red. "It's not about that. . . . I mean, sometime, maybe, but . . . I'm just talking about regular life, you know . . . just living." Boy, was I messing this up!

"I'm not sure what you mean." She looked puzzled.

"Well, like for instance . . ." I looked down at my ring. "If I have a secret, and I can't tell it, is it all right to keep the secret?"

Mom thought a moment. "That depends. Usually secrets are meant to be kept, and they should be, unless it means that someone could be hurt by it. In that case, I think you'd have to weigh the pros and cons and decide what would cause the least harm.''

''Yeah, I see what you mean.'' I thought of the magic plunging us back four hundred years in time. There was no question that Stephen or I could have been hurt. We only wanted to find his sister, but look what happened! Since I owned the ring, I'd better try to be more careful how I used it.

After a long silence Mom said, ''Jenny, is there anything you want to tell me?''

''Yes!'' I blurted out. It would be so easy to tell her everything and let her figure out what was the right thing to do. But that meant losing the magic forever. ''No! Yes, I do, but I *can't.*''

''My guess is that it's about a secret, right?'' Mom said gently.

I nodded. ''I wish I could tell you . . . but . . . do you trust me anyway?''

She thought a moment. ''Yes, I do. I trust you to make the right decision.''

''Thanks.'' That made me feel awfully good. But it also meant that now I had a huge responsibility.

Up in my room, I dug out Ophelia's letter, hoping it might help. By now, there was only that one sentence I didn't understand. *And while the Way is forged by exigency, take care not to abuse the path for Nancy's* [or *Candy's*] *sake.*

In spite of my great-grandmother's annoying habit of using the most difficult words she could find, I understood the first half. Exigency meant a strong need or want, like when I desperately wanted to see if I could visit Stephen in England. So my need sort of created a path to England. It looked like once the path was made, I could use it over and over again, except for Ophelia's warning in the second half of the sentence.

What was "Nancy's sake"? Or "Candy's sake"? The word was smudged, hard to read because it was in the crease of the paper. Nancy or Candy didn't make sense. Could it be "Fancy's sake"? I pulled out my dictionary. One meaning of *fancy* was whim or caprice. Fortunately they used it in a sentence: *to strike one's fancy*.

I tried it out in my own sentence. "I have a fancy to hop over to England." Yes, it fit. So Ophelia's warning meant: Be careful not to use the ring too often just for the heck of it.

I climbed into bed, so tired I could barely move. I lay between the soft clean sheets, weighing the pros and cons, as Mom had suggested, but couldn't decide. Should I go to Ireland tomorrow? Or should I stay home while Stephen, Margaret, and Pat went looking for the McSheehy treasure?

They were expecting me, but if I didn't show up, Stephen would guess I'd run into problems and he'd understand. He knew where the cave was, so I didn't *really* have to be there. Was wanting to go only a "fancy"?

But how could I bear to miss the moment when the McSheehy harp emerged into daylight after four hundred years underground?

chapter fourteen

School dragged by all morning. The only good news was that our basketball game against Stamford was cancelled because they were predicting a sleet storm that afternoon. I spent math, English, and science classes wondering if it was right for me to go back to Ireland. Was it only a "fancy" to want to be there when they found the treasure?

Before homeroom, and during gym class while Carly and I waited for our turns on the trampoline and parallel bars, I'd told her what had happened in Ireland. I had to keep shushing her because she kept going, "Awwk" every two seconds. She sounds a lot like a penguin when she does that.

The public library is just down the street from our school, so at lunchtime Carly and I got a pass, claiming we needed to research our science project.

It didn't take long to find a book about Irish castles. Mostly it described the famous ones, like Bunratty and

Blarney, but in the back we found a section that had notes on all the minor castles, including the McSheehys'.

When I read the comments, I said, "Carly, I *have* to show this to Stephen."

She read the short section. "That's so cool! Yeah, you should tell him, for sure."

Then an idea hit me, making me break out in goose bumps. I explained it to Carly.

"Oh wow!" Her blue eyes grew huge. "That is totally awesome. Jenny, you have to go back to Ireland. This is too big for a letter, or even a phone call."

"Your house?" I asked. "The minute school's out?"

"Okay, but on one condition." She closed the book with a thump. "You've gotta tell me *everything* the second you get back. You can't keep me hanging like that again."

"Deal," I said. "No problem."

As soon as the last bell rang, we raced through the sleet to Carly's house. I curled up in her closet and pulled out Margaret's picture of the castle and thought about the harp.

Moments later I sat on the rocky ground in front of the ruins. It was a cold Irish morning, with the huge sky above me deep blue and the sun playing hide-and-seek with puffy white clouds. Bonnie Girl was grazing near a flock of sheep. I went over and patted her. She was so glad to see me she even stopped eating for half a second.

The black rental car drove up a few minutes later, with Stephen leaning out the window, waving to me.

I went over to help pry Pat out of the backseat. The crutches emerged first, then the cast covering his toes to his knee, then the rest of him.

"Hi, Pat," I said. "Looks like you stuck your foot in a barrel of plaster."

"That's what it feels like too," he grumbled, pulling himself up onto the crutches. "What a fuss over a couple of lousy broken bones."

"Don't mind him," Stephen told me. "He's in a mood because the doctor refuses to let him hike up into the mountains with us."

"I could manage okay," Pat insisted. "If he'd used one of those new lightweight casts like I wanted—"

"Don't listen to him, Jenny," Margaret said. "He made quite a job of his ankle and the doctor did what he had to do. He said, and I quote, 'Patrick McSheehy, you'll not be leaping about like a mountain goat for quite a time to come, so you might as well make your peace with it.' "

"Some nurse you are," Pat said. "Where's the sympathy? Where's the tender loving care you women are supposed to show us brave wounded soldiers?"

Margaret grinned. "You'll have it when you promise to behave yourself."

"Just bring me my harp, woman, that's all I ask." He hobbled over to a stone wall and sat down with a grimace of pain.

"That's what we intend to do," Stephen said. "And the sooner we start, the sooner we'll return. Ready, Jenny?"

"All set." I tucked the library book between two stones in the wall.

"What's that?" he asked.

"A book I'll show you later. Right now let's go find treasure!"

We started off across the fields, Stephen wearing the backpack stuffed with supplies for any emergency—just in case.

Now that we knew exactly where to head, we figured it would take us less than an hour to reach the cave, and that turned out to be about right. The stream that flowed from the waterfall had changed its course, but the outline of the mountains remained the same, and so did the ravine, although it was deeper and the rocky ledge overhanging it was gone.

We climbed up and up, and I finally spotted the boulder that hid the cave entrance. Even with the pine trees gone, I recognized the spot right away.

I jogged toward it, followed by the others. "This is it," I called over my shoulder. "Now, let's just hope . . ." I circled around the boulder. "Yes, the cave's still here!" I whooped.

"Why wouldn't it be?" Margaret asked. "You saw it only last night."

"Oh!" I said, startled. "Did I say 'cave'? I meant 'treasure.' I hope the *treasure's* in here."

She stooped down. "It's quite low, isn't it? Rather . . . confining . . ."

"Do small spaces give you the creeps?" I asked.

She nodded. "I'm afraid so. I'm sorry, it's always been a problem."

"Don't worry," Stephen said. "I'll go in." He took off the backpack, removed the flashlight from it, then knelt down and began to crawl inside. I felt excitement rise in me like a balloon. After all these years the treasure would finally be uncovered.

Stephen's feet were still sticking out when he called in a muffled voice, "I can't go any farther. The walls have partly collapsed at one point along here and my shoulders won't fit through the opening."

"Can you back out?" I asked. "My shoulders aren't as wide. I'll try if you want."

He crawled out, covered with dirt. "There's quite a way to go, Jenny. From what I could see, the cave must run twelve feet or more back into the mountain."

"Okay." I took the flashlight he handed me and knelt down, then lowered myself onto my belly. Shining the beam in front of me, I saw the rockslide that had narrowed the cave to about a two-foot diameter.

I backed out, took off my jacket, and started over. I was wearing school clothes, including my favorite yellow sweater, but even if it ended up ruined, any sacrifice was worth it. I was going to rescue the McSheehy treasure!

Inching my way along, I saw that the cave turned at an angle shortly after the narrow spot. I made it through, my shoulders scraping against the rock. Riiip. There went my sweater.

The roof was less than a foot over my head. Margaret would definitely not like it in here.

The flashlight picked up a jumble of rocks ahead. Beyond the pile I could see nothing. Under the rocks, an edge of fabric showed. I reached out and felt it. It was a scrap of the red blanket Alainn had wrapped around the harp.

It's still here! I thought. But buried under stones. This didn't look good.

I aimed the flashlight beam up. The roof of the cave was now almost four feet above me. The stones that had been up there had fallen to the ground. Getting to my knees, I peered over the rockpile.

Nothing. An empty space about a few feet square, ending in a solid wall. No bags of gold and jewels, only dust and dirt and more stones.

One by one, I threw the heap of rocks into the empty space at the rear of the cave. Slowly I uncovered the woolen cloth. It was eaten away in spots, revealing the rotting leather harp bag.

It looked much too flat.

I removed the last stones. There was no trace of the jewelry. No gold, no rubies, no pearls. They must have been taken sometime over the last four hundred years. I hoped it was by a farm kid like Mickey, someone who needed the money.

But the harp bag was left. Did they remove the harp and leave the bag?

I propped the flashlight on the ground and tried to open it. The rotting leather shredded at my touch. I pulled the scraps apart.

There was the harp. Smashed into zillions of pieces.

I felt sick. I remembered how Alainn had handled the harp so gently, had coaxed such beautiful music from it, how she had loved it. Now it was only splinters.

I pulled off my sweater and carefully eased the remains of the red cloth, bag, and harp onto it, trying not to disturb the fragments any more than I could help. Wrapping the edges together, I backed up, slowly dragging the bundle after me down the long tunnel.

I'd only gone a couple of feet when the flashlight beam picked up the gleam of a tiny circle. I grabbed it out of the dirt and brushed it off. It was a pearl! One single pearl. I scrabbled around in the loose earth for the entire length of the tunnel but found no more.

As I neared the entrance I realized that Stephen had been calling my name for some time.

"I'm okay!" I shouted. "I'm coming." I backed out into daylight.

"Did you find the harp?" Margaret asked. "Was it—" She spotted the bundle.

"I'm sorry." I unfolded the sweater. Neither of them said a word as they gazed at the crushed harp.

In the sunlight, we saw that some of the wood had been nibbled by insects and other bits had rotted into powder.

After a while Margaret whispered, "Pat will be so disappointed."

"It's a terrible shame, isn't it?" Stephen said.

"I'm sorry," I repeated. "That's all that was left. And this." I gave her the pearl. "The rest of the jewels are gone."

After a moment Stephen straightened his shoulders. "Well, it can't be helped. We did our best. Four hundred years is a long time."

"Yes, it is." I looked at him and knew we were both thinking of Alainn and the last time we stood in this spot, listening to her fill the air with music.

"Right," Margaret said. "We'd better start back."

It was a quiet walk down the mountain.

When Pat saw us coming, he struggled up on his crutches. Margaret carried the bundle cradled in her arms like a baby. She shook her head when she saw Pat's eager face. He slumped back down on the rock wall and waited until we reached him.

"The ceiling of the cave collapsed," I said as she handed him her package.

He unwrapped the sweater and bit his lip when he saw the fragments. He was silent as I explained what I'd found.

"The bags of jewels are gone," Stephen added. "But Jenny found one pearl."

Margaret held it out, but Pat only glanced at it. "Who cares about jewels," he growled. He picked up two scraps of wood. Studying them closely, he brought them together. They fit. He picked up a third and a fourth. They didn't quite match.

"It will probably never play music again," he said. "And it won't be of value to anyone but me, but this is the McSheehy harp. It will take time, but I can piece it back together—what remains of it."

"That's right." Margaret sat down next to him on the wall. The pearl in her hand glowed in the sunshine. "And you'll be able to tell your family that the old legend is true. The lost McSheehy treasure does exist."

"Yes," Pat said. "And I'm holding it in my hands." A look of wonder filled his face.

They began talking quietly. I picked up the library book

from its crevice and led Stephen over to the distant field where Bonnie Girl grazed.

"Stephen, it's only a short history, but this tells us what happened to the McSheehys after the battle. Plus, there's an incredible little note in here."

"What does it say?" he asked.

"I'll read it to you in a minute, but first let me tell you about the war." I opened the book to my place mark. "The English won the battle. Donogh, the *rí,* was killed in the fighting, even though we tried to warn him, but his brothers survived, and just like the legend says, they and Finnin argued over who would become the new king."

"Who won?" Stephen asked.

"Alainn." I grinned. "She got fed up with all the bickering, named Finnin the heir, and made herself his regent. That meant that she actually became the ruler because Finnin wasn't much interested in the hard work of being king. The book says, 'He frittered his life away with games and drink while his grandmother ran his domain.' "

"So that means the castle wasn't destroyed by the English?" he asked.

"Not then. It was 'too remote and unimportant,' the book says, for Queen Elizabeth's troops to bother with. It was wrecked by Oliver Cromwell—the Puritan guy you told me about—much later. By then, Alainn had died of old age and the McSheehys were 'divided into warring factions,' as the book puts it, and none of them were powerful enough to rebuild the castle."

"I'm glad Alainn lived a long life, even if it wasn't

always a happy one," Stephen said. "What happened to Marra?"

"Here's the incredible part!" I said. "Let me read it to you. 'One odd story concerns Lady Alainn and her daughter-in-law, Lady Marra. Both were known as wisewomen, or witches, for their knowledge of healing herbs and second sight—' What is 'second sight'?" I asked.

"Seeing things others can't. Such as the way Alainn looked at you and knew right away about your magic."

"Right." I continued reading, " 'It's not known how they came upon the idea, but they exhibited quite advanced knowledge for the times. They regularly performed a so-called magical rite several times a year. All rushes were removed from the castle and burned, clothes and bedding were washed, and the floors and walls of the castle scrubbed down. They also practiced the then-peculiar habit of washing their hands before eating or handling food. These precautions led to unprecedented standards of sanitation, and the McSheehys became well-known for their robust good health in a time when many sickened and died early in life.' "

"That was your idea, Jenny." He patted me on the back. "Good for you."

"Wait, there's more. 'The McSheehys, almost alone in the area, avoided the devastating effects of the great plague. The plague, of course, was carried by fleas, and the periodic cleaning of the castle greatly reduced the incidence of this terrible disease. As a result, both Lady Alainn and Lady Marra became celebrated for their magical witchcraft powers, and were honored with great devotion by all their subjects for the remainder of their lives.' "

"That's simply super," Stephen said. "They deserved it too."

"I may have given them the idea," Jenny said. "But they were the ones who listened and did what I suggested. I'm really happy for them."

"So am I."

"But you know what, Stephen?" The idea had been giving me shivers ever since I found the book in the library. "You, Margaret, and Pat are all McSheehys. You're related to the people in the castle. What if we hadn't gone back in time? And what if Alainn and Marra didn't decide to practice the 'American magic' cleaning rituals?"

"I think I can guess what you're getting at." His voice rose with excitement.

I nodded. "Maybe the McSheehy who was your ancestor would have died of the plague, or some other disease, before he—or she—got married and had children. Maybe that son or daughter would never have been born. . . ."

"And that would mean that we—Margaret, Pat, and myself—would not have been born. We simply wouldn't exist."

We looked at each other. Finally he said, "It's scary to think about, isn't it?"

"Yes, but it makes me feel good too. It's like our trip back to the castle was meant to happen," I whispered. "Maybe we were supposed to be there."

"It's a lot to think about, isn't it?" Stephen said.

"Yes."

We stood quietly together for a while, looking at the

ruins of the castle rearing up against the crisp blue sky.

"I'm glad we went," I said at last.

"Me too." He glanced over at Pat and Margaret, who were bent over the harp, then he leaned forward and gently, sweetly, kissed me. On the mouth.

I felt tingles ripple through me, all the way down to my toes. His arms went around me and I held him tight. He'd hugged me often, when we were both so scared, so far from home, but this was different. This hug meant yes, we were good, good friends, and yes, we were more than good friends too. I pulled back and looked into his dark soft eyes, and it was all there, spoken without words.

Bonnie Girl chose that moment to push her head between us and nicker. I laughed and rubbed her ears.

"How would you like to have a new owner, Bonnie?" I asked her. "I'm thinking of leaving a note for Mickey, telling him he now has a horse to ride on his trips from the valley."

"Good idea, Jenny," Stephen said. "And perhaps we can come back once in a while for a good fast canter on her."

"No thanks." I grinned. "Horses aren't my thing. Besides . . ." I looked off at the mountains. He'd be disappointed, but I couldn't help it. "I have to stop hopping back and forth across the ocean so often, Stephen."

"What's the matter?" he asked.

I told him about my talk with Mom last night and finished by saying, "So I won't be able to just pop over for a cup of tea whenever I feel like it."

"I understand, and I think you're right." He took my

hands. "Letters, and perhaps an occasional phone call, are good enough for ordinary people. Why not us?"

"Yes, why not us?" I felt I could gaze into those dark eyes forever. "But, of course, I'll come see you on special occasions . . . birthdays . . . the first day of school vacation . . . the *last* day of school vacation . . . Christmas, for sure . . ."

"Of course!" He laughed, startling Bonnie Girl, who snorted and trotted off. "Come on, I'll race you to the castle!"

We ran through the fields under the wide Irish sky, whooping and shouting with joy.

Dear *Anywhere* Readers Everywhere,

Miracles sometimes happen when you least expect them, and when you let your imagination fly free, you and Jenny may find yourselves in places—and times—where you least expect to be.

In the next adventure, *Lost Valley*, the surprises and discoveries spring from Davy's experiments with the magical ring. Jenny's been hoping her little brother doesn't understand how the ring is connected with the magic, but he's a lot smarter than she realizes. Except he doesn't *quite* get it right and before they know it, Jenny, Davy, and Carly are whirled back in time to the Old West!

They land on a ranch in the Colorado Rocky Mountains, where Ophelia Anne Cavanaugh lives. But Jenny's great-grandmother has not yet become the old lady who wrote the say-nothing letter. It's 1906 and she's only thirteen. *And* she, too, has just inherited the magical ring.

However, Ophelia is . . . different, to put it politely, and Jenny finds she can be a total *pain* sometimes.

But Jenny, Carly and Davy love the ranch, the Rockies, and the simple pioneer life. Soon after they arrive, they ride their horses through a meadow of wildflowers and meet a blond, blue-eyed young cowboy who lives just beyond Hawk Peak. He's really cute—and he can't keep his eyes off Carly!

When Ophelia leads them to a valley hidden deep in the mountains, Jenny falls in love with the beauty of this untouched wilderness. Wading in the clear (icy!) creek, she spots a glittery pebble in the water and picks it up. Are those flecks of *real gold*?

You'll find out when we meet again in Colorado! See you in *Lost Valley!*

Louise Ladd